TALL TREES SHORT STORIES
VOLUME 21

TALL TREES
SHORT STORIES

VOLUME 21

GABRIEL HEMERY

WOOD WIDE WORKS

Cover design by Gabriel Hemery, incorporating brush design from
Ki-Cek on Deviant Art.

This edition first published in March 2021.

Wood Wide Works
www.woodwide.works

ISBN ebook: 9781916336223
ISBN paperback: 9781916336230

FOR MY FAITHFUL WRITING COMPANIONS:

To Persephone, for early morning contemplations and heart-warming affection;
To Bizou, for inspiring walks and untiring belief in my mastery.

Contents

AUTHOR'S NOTE

I was surprised and delighted by reactions from readers and reviewers to my first collection of environmental tales in Tall Trees Short Stories: Volume 20. I had also surprised myself by how much I enjoyed writing short stories.

During 2020, I decided to write a story every month of the year and to release these to regular readers via my newsletter. This public promise to my wonderful readers was sometimes tough to fulfil yet proved to be a great discipline. The more I wrote, the more my writing developed, gaining in mellifluousness and perhaps a flourish of concinnity!

Volume 21 of Tall Trees Short Stories includes some stories that I have already shared with my readers but also many more that will be new to everyone. Personally, I think that this new collection features some of my better stories, but of course the truth lies in the reading. Much as I am humbled in the face of nature, I remain humbled in the eyes of my readers.

Gabriel Hemery
January 2021

FIN

2044

❧

LE DÉBUT DE LA FIN

As in all good beginnings, the end is out of sight, except as it is in this case, when the end is the beginning. My story for you begins on what will be my last day on Earth, at the onset of the final moments of a fragile life. Here I am talking with you. Some would think this a privilege, others a curse, but until you know more of my story you may want to hold onto any judgement a moment longer. I know you must look at me and wonder whether there is much of a story that can be told by a body which can move only its lips, whose face is so unpleasant to focus on while you struggle to hear its faint whisper.

Do you have time to listen now? Really, then, if you are sure.

Tomorrow evening I was to reach my one hundredth year, but you and I both know the full day will not come for me. When you watch the sky lighten before sunrise and you hear the joy of the song thrush which has heralded every day for me beyond my window; share a last breath with me. When you draw the blinds to filter the sun's first rays and notice the dew glittering along the shadowed fringes of the wood; remember our conversation. When later you leave this place for your home and watch the bees busy on the lime flowers and the brimstone butterflies darting through the fire of the evening sun, spare a warm thought for me. I don't expect you to remember me past tomorrow. Why would you? You say so many final farewells to lonely old people like me, you must have become as tough as treeum.

For me, this time there is no escape from love and loss, no saviour

2

from the chilling Seine or a charging sanglier, no more epic battles with a mighty châtaignier or with either of the big Cs. Only the final escape from a ravaged body and the end of a life that may never have been at all. For me it is le début de la fin.

Now, where shall I begin?

2021

࿇

'If you don't like "Space Putty", then what do you think we should call it?' That was the simple challenge thrown back at me by a lab colleague 30 years ago.

'I think it should honour the fact that it's tree-based that's all,' I replied. 'Something like tree putty or tree ... um, or maybe there's a French—' And just like that, from the void of my non-marketeer's brain, came the name for the world's most famous miracle material; Treeum™.

Ah, from your intake of breath I think that you know who I am now, even though you and most people have never known my name. That's the way I've always wanted it to be. My anonymity has allowed me to live a normal life despite the many impediments I've faced, but at least the trappings of fame have not tripped me up. Although I cannot imagine how a man with so severe a disfigurement could ever be lauded by society.

As a young man I was fortunate to gain a scholarship to study engineering at university. It was one the few lucky breaks of my life which otherwise has dealt me ... well, I may tell more in a moment. Young people from my arrondissement, my district, had the chance to apply for a scholarship if they met certain criteria, and it's fair to say that I met all of these: no parents to speak of, low income, high potential for criminality, but with a modicum of natural ability. You can imagine my circumstances perhaps? Yet fate had other ideas and I never graduated. In fact, I didn't even complete my first term, despite finishing top of the class in the first assignment. It was no fault of Édith, nor of my infatuation with her, simply circumstance. I am not a good advertisement to young people who are told they must go to university to be successful in life, but then I am here only because of a series of natural accidents.

When you can no longer walk, you must seek new ways to gain freedom. When you lose your sight, you are as vulnerable as a new-born babe abandoned in a dark forest. After my rebirth, paralysed and blinded following a beastly attack, I began a journey of self-discovery in search of nascent senses. Eventually, my medical treatment and intellectual adventures coalesced to bring me to Britain and here to Oxfordshire; the home of world-leading health care and epicentre of bioscience technology start-ups.

The labs were on the outskirts of Oxford city, the futuristic building set among a large coniferous plantation. Pine trees not only smell good but sing like no other tree; did you know that? On a windy day—and it always blows because the country is so flat—the creaking branches, whistling needles and falling cones, accompanied by the scampering claws of squirrels and the cooing of doves, created a musical drama worthy of Gustave Charpentier. I suppose I should compare it to your Elgar? Every morning when I arrived for work, I'd wheel my chair to the back of the car park and take a moment to enjoy the performance. Sometimes I would dream that I was clinging to the top of a swaying pine and a previous life, feeling the thrill of the wind and gazing across their needled tips to the dreaming spires beyond. Of course, it was something I'd never seen, and it may not even be possible to see the spires of Oxford from there, but when I asked my colleagues, they had no idea either. I suspect none of them ever stopped between their cars and the labs and wouldn't know a pine from a fir if you poked them with a sharpened branch of either.

Treeum™ was revolutionary because it was both resistant and adaptive, dependent on the charge you gave the material. Used in airplane wings it adapts to rapid changes in air pressure to smooth the flight for passengers, or with the flick of a switch it will change the wing profile of a fighter jet to suit a mission or to combat a sudden threat. In construction it has enabled architects to design earthquake-resistant buildings, and the construction of super skyscrapers made entirely with wood and other carbon-neutral materials. Naturally, it has always pleased me that the main constituent of Treeum™ is tree cellulose, and that I've played a small part in helping another miracle of the natural world make human society a little bit more sustainable.

In 2021, my ravaged body took another hit. I was diagnosed with testicular cancer. While I recovered in hospital following an orchidectomy—a strangely feminine name for such an emasculating term don't you think?—the other big C continued to swirl around the world. Victims younger, fitter, and more worthy than me dropped like windblown spruce trees on a mountain ridge. Lives of those caring for me toppled one after the other. I would barely get to know a nurse before he or she would disappear. 'Gone into self-isolation,' I'd be told, and I knew better than to ask of them in the weeks afterwards. And then the virus found me.

1944

❧

The two girls skipped hand-in-hand along the narrow winding lane, the white heads of cow parsley stretching high above their heads. 'Keep off the road,' she'd said, but they were confident they'd hear any Germans coming and have time to hide, and anyway, it was a thrill defying their mother. Anne had heard the rumour of more killings in the village the other side of the hill the day before, together with thrilling whispers of the Allies coming soon to free them.

Anne pulled her younger sister Lucie behind her as they ran giggling from the lane and headed across the meadow towards the wood at the top of the hill. Anne was much more grown up now and promised her mum to be helpful by looking out for wild garlic. Last time the girls had been in the woods together they had built a tank out of chestnut branches and sat inside eating dry bread coated with freshly made confiture des mûres which they'd spread with their fingers. They had sucked their sticky fingertips savouring the sweetness before wiping them on their dresses. That had been the previous autumn and now they were ten and eight. Anne thought that Lucie was finally becoming just a little bit less annoying.

Suddenly, a huge brown shaggy dog came into sight. A deep growl escaped from between its bared white teeth, and he backed away to stand guard over something, someone, on the forest floor. Anne and Lucie had seen many dead bodies, even if the grown-ups had always attempted to shield their eyes. The woman in front of them was definitely dead. She was as white as a ghost and sat in a strange way, slumped against the trunk of a big tree. There was a lot of blood staining the pleats of her pretty dress.

Neither of the girls screamed, but Lucie began to cry and squeezed her older sister's hand tightly while they both looked nervously from the dog to the body. As they stood frozen to the spot, their feet buried deep in chestnut leaves where they'd come to an abrupt halt, a small bundle stirred in the forest floor and wailed like its life depended on it. That was the moment when both girls screamed.

1982

I've always felt a certain affinity with the châtaignier, the sweet chestnut. You could say she was my … my sage-femme, how do you say it, my middle wife? We have known each a long time, but this particular specimen was new to me. She was in her middle age, getting a little round around her waist you could say, but still full of life. She'd had the misfortune of being struck by lightning the previous summer and one half of her once spreading crown had been charred to its core. It so happened that her weakened side leaned over a woodland ride popular with families, so the lady of the château regrettably came to the decision that it must be removed. She enjoyed nature and appreciated that the tree was the favourite instrument for a black woodpecker to practise his drumming on to impress his mate.

Having escaped the grime of the city and its now lifeless charms, I'd been working as an arborist for more than 15 years. I was regularly invited to conduct tree surgery on the specimen cedars in the garden near the château and to work on special trees elsewhere on the estate. The foresters would manage the 200-year-long rotations of oak which was the tradition of the family, whose giant trees were felled for cooperage and other crafts. The family were active hunters, enjoying regular red meats from cerf and sanglier … you know, deer and boar. Nonetheless, I was surprised to hear the horn and the dogs in full voice while I unpacked my bag containing ropes, carabiners, and helmet. I could make out their continued excitement in the distance as I began to sharpen the chain of my saw. It was early in the season, but I knew there were too many sanglier in the woods. Last winter a walker was lucky to escape with his life, but on three separate occasions dogs had been gored and killed. It is their défense you know, those big teeth they have in their lower jaw that can rip you open like a sack of marrons.

I was thinking about the marrons, the chestnuts, while I climbed the big tree because they are the favourite food of the sanglier. I caught myself wondering what the big boar might think if he saw me climbing his precious larder, but then I told myself I was stupid because a sanglier cannot see a human figure much more than 15 metres away.

A châtaignier is a hard tree to climb because its branches don't spread out, flat and even like a cedar, but reach for the sky in great twisting vertical columns. The dead and dying wood would make the job all the more difficult and I knew that I must concentrate on where I tied myself on and where I placed my feet. My top-handled chainsaw dangled below me on a rope fixed to my waist allowing me to use all my limbs to climb freely.

Despite the dangers I loved my job, and nothing was better than the sway of a tree when you reached the top of its crown, or the spectacular views across the top of a forest and the glorious French campagne beyond. We were supposed to work in pairs for safety, but that day my buddy was ill and I took the decision to continue alone. It was only a short job after all. I made my way carefully out across the severely damaged crown of the châtaignier and began my work. I had left warning signs on the path below to tell walkers to keep away, but still I shouted out a warning before I allowed a cut to fall, just in case.

I finished sawing through another large branch and turned off the engine of my chainsaw in readiness to let the heavy limb drop. 'Attention!' I shouted, as my fingers loosened their grip on the rope. At that exact moment something travelled across my lower orbit. A jogger appeared, dressed all in black, lost in her own little world generated by her white earbuds. Her red hair flowed like a comet, looking uncannily like my Édith. In shock and panic I grabbed for the already accelerating limb, but I was too late. I lost my balance and realised as I followed the limb in horrific slow motion that I should have stopped falling long ago. I had made a fatal mistake with my anchor rope.

I remember crashing headfirst through a swirl of branches and watching the brown forest floor rushing to meet me. I wondered if it would hurt, and stupidly whether the châtaignier leaves might soften my fall.

I don't know how it happened exactly, but I regained consciousness, not among the nurturing leaves, but dangling upside-down just above them. My blood-filled head pulsated angrily, and I stretched an arm to try to touch the ground, but my fingers only brushed the serrated margins of a few leaves framing the edge of the muddy path. Then I made the mistake of attempting to move my waist and I remember only excruciating agony before I must have passed out again.

I dreamt of red-haired heavenly bodies but woke to unparalleled pain shooting through my hips and legs. I realised that I may have dislocated my pelvis and raised my head slowly to look at my feet. I was amazed to see my two legs trussed up like a cerf swinging in my mistress's game larder. I remembered that I had an emergency knife in a sheath on my belt but realised that there was no hope I could ever reach the rope to cut myself free. There was no sight of the jogger. I admit that tears came then; tears of pain, embarrassment, and regret. Then, in the distance, the sound of approaching dogs and shouting. Relief washed over me, and more tears flowed over my forehead.

Panicked snorts of 'ukh! ukh!' accompanied a tremendous crashing through the undergrowth, and the baying of the dogs reached a crescendo close behind. A giant boar skidded to a sudden halt five metres away and locked his eyes onto mine before delving into my soul. He shook his massive head, which made up almost half his bristling hulk, as if trying to make sense of the enemy confronting him. He sniffed the air and with a snarl of the lips either side of his huge tusks, charged straight towards my head.

1963

∾

Michael had heard the rumours of another protest march but he hadn't thought they would march the same route again, and certainly not cross the bridge where so many had been hurt just weeks before. He'd been sitting on the pontoon talking with Chloe, his girlfriend of two years and fellow student of medicine at the University of Paris. They watched the peaceful but noisy protest move past them over the bridge. Without warning, panic seem to erupt among the protestors and the crowd tried to fold back on itself just as riot police came into view at the head of the bridge.

The two observers gaped up in horror as the banner-wielding front rank of protestors fell under a storm of vicious raining batons. When the screaming began, Michael jumped to his feet in alarm, watching the police smash their way forward. His eye was drawn to one couple who he thought must be together because the man was trying to protect his friend. The woman fell to the ground, the victim of a vicious truncheon strike, and then unbelievably, while one policeman struck the guy repeatedly round the head, two colleagues pushed him against the parapet and then tipped him over the side. The man fell like a ragdoll, his arms trailing behind him as he tumbled face-first into the Seine.

With Chloe's screams and pleading echoing through his mind,

Michael stripped off his shoes and coat, and jumped into the chilly waters and began to swim out towards the body which lay face down and half-submerged. Someone had thrown a lifebuoy and with relief Michael managed to reach it, tucking one of own his arms through the ring and grasping the lifeless body with his other. His girlfriend now shouted encouragement from the shore and three guys began pulling hard on the rope attached to the ring. The two of them reached the safety of the pontoon and strong hands pulled them both out of the dark water.

Michael had never had to revive a real patient before, but his training kicked in and he worked with Chloe to clear the man's lungs of water. It was only later, when the adrenalin faded, that he thought about what had happened and his whole body shook uncontrollably. He hoped the young man would make it. At least he was now in the hands of the medics. He wondered if the young woman next to the man when the police charged forward had been as fortunate.

1963

❧

When we met, she was wearing a simple black dress, its round neck cut low enough to expose exquisite clavicles and a dull jewel hanging from a plain necklace. Our two groups of friends had gathered round a too-small table in my favourite cafe in the poor arrondissement where I lived and worked evenings while pretending to study at the overcrowded lecture halls of the University of Paris.

Compared to the cardigans and frilly blouses of the familiar girls in my group, Édith beckoned me from my stormy life like the million-candle-power lamp of a lighthouse. Her red hair shone like an aura in the gloomy back room. I knew with a burning intensity, despite having never loved before—even as my nineteen-year-old eyes travelled from her neck and sailed into her eyes—that we would become passionate lovers.

We'd gathered to plan a sit-in at the university but ended up discussing the brutality of the police against the Algerians. Not that any of it mattered to me at that moment. My breath seemed to have been taken away, and it took all my powers of concentration to save myself from being blinded by staring at her too much. There was a male hand around her waist, but it mattered little. This was meant to be. We were meant to be. Her soul had already burned itself onto the back of my eyes.

La Mère Catherine restaurant had become almost my second home since I fled the brutality of the orphanage at the eastern fringes of the city. It shared its name with my mother. Sipping her blood in its dark back room had become a religion, whether I shared the bottle with friends, or cried silently and alone while diving into the deep end of the wine.

I slipped my hand into Édith's as we walked along the bank of the Seine under the skeletal pollarded trees of platane à feuilles d'érable. Sorry, I don't know their English name, but as their name tells you they have maple-like leaves. You have many of them also in London. Edith's boyfriend didn't notice at first, even though he held her other hand in his. We stopped just short of the three arches of Pont Saint-Michel—where two weeks before hundreds had been pushed or leapt into the river to escape police brutality—in readiness to part ways, when he finally noticed. He looked with incomprehension at our clasped hands, and while his frown deepened, his shocked eyes moved to her face. Not a word had been spoken, but Édith and I looked at him in unison while her fingers clasped mine invisibly tighter. He hesitated, unsure for a moment whether to fight or flee, but in his heart and mind he knew the truth. He would never win this battle, not against an opponent with my reputation for toughness. He turned his back and walked away from us through a fluttering shower of leaves stirred from the Parisian platanes by the autumnal breeze.

Over the next two weeks Édith and I were inseparable, rarely out of bed and never far from passion. Only hunger and exhaustion dragged us away from her flat. I must surely have lost my job but that was furthest from my mind. We were lovesick patients inside the iron filigree of her balcony, and outside the rain-smeared window, each day the platane trees completed more of their slow striptease. I'd watch their leaves fall and flutter while Édith's chest rose and beat under my ear, her hand stroking my hair and her soft breasts feeding my soul.

News of the funeral of the little sparrow, La Môme Piaf, finally woke us from our revelry, and we joined thousands of others parading the rain-soaked streets, watching in wonder at the complete absence of the usual static Parisian traffic. Piaf was apparently the namesake for my Édith, the knowledge of which stirred only morbid thoughts. We returned to the flat and listened to 'Le Chant d'amour' while we wiped tears from each other's eyes.

'Our two lovers, our two crazy in love
They both died of the same sadness
So, let me cry...'

Next day we gathered once again at La Mère Catherine, and it struck me then that I'd been fully weaned off her by Édith. Talk was of the Algerians again and a major march was in the planning. Halfway through the evening, Édith and I sloped off to the toilets to relieve ourselves, and when we returned to the group their blood was up. News of further brutality by the police and that fucking Gestapo Papon and his FPA militia spread rapidly among the tables. By the end of the night, sometime in the early hours, a battle plan had been prepared to fight the injustice of the curfew against our fellow French citizens.

A week later we joined with five thousand others at Grands Boulevards and until we reached Opéra we walked hand-in-hand in peaceful protest. We heard fighting break out in the front ranks and looked nervously ahead. Édith sat on my shoulders but still couldn't see clearly over all the placards. Then a surge of people pushed back from the front and a ripple of screaming rushed towards us. We were swept back towards the river as the smell of tear gas spread through the crowd and the noise of water cannon grew closer. Then came the unmistakable sound of gunfire.

We were swept onto the Pont Saint-Michel and impossibly Édith and I suddenly found ourselves at the front facing a charge of riot police. I turned my back towards them hoping my backpack would protect me and as I reached sideways to protect Édith I watched in slow motion as a truncheon cracked her skull and the helmet of another simultaneously smashed into her face. My shout of 'Non!' was silenced by a glancing blow from a baton and before I could make sense of the world, I watched the riverside platanes tumble and spin, the grey of the autumn sky blurring alternatively with the brown of the Seine.

1982

❧

Their quarry should have been out of sight by now, not circling around and tearing into something hanging over the path with its hideous tusks. Even the dogs had stopped in their tracks. The pair of griffon nivernais stood panting by the woman's side, growling deeply with their hackles raised, unsure what to do.

Instinctively, Valerie de Normande raised the beautifully-figured walnut of the rifle butt to her tweed-padded shoulder. Ignoring the sanglier's huge blood-splattered head and the subject of its rage which swung to and fro, in and out of her sights, she aimed one-third up its deep chest directly above the elbow of its foreleg. She took what was undoubtedly the best and perhaps riskiest shot of her hunting life.

1944

※

Our hamlet was of little consequence to the Nazi forces who briefly paused to decimate it during their northward rush through the June countryside. Its tiny size and relatively few victims meant that it never gained the notoriety of Tulle and Oradour-sur-Glane.

My parents lived in a farmhouse sandwiched between the coast road and the wood, where we shared our dilapidated home with a few hens and Rou, our red and white Normande cow. My father was a résistance fighter, taken away by the Wehrmacht nine months previously. Since his capture my mother had lived under the threat of a widow's shadow, existing on the dwindling produce of Rou. She benefited from a daily intake of her rich creamy milk which she made into a range of home-churned products, while any leftovers she used to bargain for soap or thread. Her favourite company was our fierce and loyal Lyonette. The briard sheep dog didn't suffer fools or strangers kindly, and even the fiercest of resistance fighters passing through held a healthy respect for him. No one could creep nearer than the outermost row of apple trees in the orchard behind the kitchen garden, even in the dead of night, not without Lyonette raising the alarm.

You may wonder where my place is in this story, but please bear with me. In addition to the passing maquisards, the faithful Lyonette and generous Rou, my 23-year-old mother came to realise that she was indeed to become a mother for the first time. Waves of morning sickness disrupted her early chores around the farm and made her forget her lover and soulmate, if only briefly, before his memory would return to haunt her stronger still. She would hold her hand to her belly and imagine me, her future child, and wonder if I might be blessed with his eyes and patriotic nose, while tears rolled down her sunken cheeks.

The engine of the kübelwagen was known and feared by every French citizen, except of course by the traitors of Vichy. Favoured by staff of the Waffen-SS, it was a portent which put a fist in your belly. My mother was ripe to bursting, and struggled to eat even a little cheese, let alone being able to accommodate a Nazi fist. A deep rumbling growl from Lyonette raised the hairs on the back of her neck, and she hurried from the hen coup where she'd been cleaning and collecting the day's second batch of eggs. She hushed the dog and strained her ears, and there, sure enough, she could hear a vehicle approaching, but it was still a good mile off. Then a short burst of light machine gun fire pierced the air.

She'd been listening to Radio Londres and receiving hurried first-hand reports from excited résistance fighters. She knew the allies were coming, and Nazi fingers were already nervous on triggers even before the maquis had launched one brazen attack after another. There were rumours of vicious reprisals, and impossibly, of more cruelty than usual.

Luckily for my mother, and me, she was standing just paces away from her emergency canvas bag hidden in a roof void over the chickens. In it were a couple of tins of provisions, a candle and matches, a folding knife, a canteen filled with water, and a few rolls of bandages. Without hesitation she hurried back inside and felt for it under the corrugated tin; it was pushed back further than she thought, and a robin had built a nest of twigs and moss since she'd placed it there in the spring of the previous year. It was while she stretched and reached forward on the tips of her toes that she had her first contraction.

Survival was hardwired in my mother, and with a feat of superhuman strength she buried the pain and hurried out of the farmyard, away from her home, and up the slope towards the wood. Lyonette followed close to her heal as she struggled to reach the shadows of the verdant wild pear and plum. More gunfire, closer this time, and shouts from the direction of her neighbour's farm. She reached the wood's edge and crawled on her hands and knees through the spiny thicket, and into the darker stand of sweet chestnut, only pausing when she knew she would not be visible through a pair of standard issue field binoculars.

No one approached from the direction of her farm, but she could see vehicles and grey uniformed figures now moving in her yard. More gunfire and a roaring bellow of agony; at least Rou had not suffered long. She clasped her hands tightly over her ears, and as she watched the first wisp of smoke swirl from the ancient barn, a second and more powerful contraction took her breath away. This time she waited for it to pass completely, and as the pain eased her mind began to grapple more clearly with thoughts as to her next move. She was probably safe in the wood, she thought, as it had no strategic importance. Further in, near the coppices, stood the old woodsman's hut. She had no idea if it still had a roof and it was long-abandoned; no one had been working the wood for years. She knew that it offered a possible refuge which she now urgently needed.

She began to move further into the wood, past a tangle of dead branches that were probably a child's den. The next contraction, less than a minute later, stopped her in her tracks. My mother doubled up in pain, resting her hand against the rough spiralling bark of an ancient châtaignier. Her waters broke as she leant against the great tree and she realised then that she'd never make it to the hut. Crawling round to the other side of the tree, she nestled in between two of its large buttress roots. She leaned back and waited for the next contraction, pulling her bag onto her chest so that important things remained in reach. The tree supported her splaying legs and embraced her while she bit on a small branch to prevent her wails from betraying her.

My mother stayed there long after the Germans had left the hamlet with enough freshly butchered beef and eggs to keep the squad in luxury for several days, and with the satisfaction that there were six fewer sympathisers for the partisans. It was almost dark and crepuscular life had started to stir when I entered this world. Serenaded by a pair of waking tawny owls, my mother screeched and I wailed in unison. Lyonette stood guard, alert to every sound with one eye on his mistress, the other on the woods.

A dark fluttering cloud of feeding horseshoe bats circled overhead as she lifted me to her breast. I seemed to have a strong will to survive and took readily to her, remaining firmly latched on, even while she added one rolled bandage after another to stem the flow of blood from between her legs. Her last act was to cut the cord which bonded us together, before swaddling me in her farm apron, using its waist ties to bind me tightly. She lost consciousness soon afterward and her soul slipped silently from her bloodless body into the silvan night.

Eventually, I rolled from her lifeless arms to land face down among the sharp-edged chestnut leaves and its prickly husks. I inhaled the earthy forest which stilled my wailing through the rest of the night until a song thrush joined me in pronouncing that another day had come.

2021

Sylvie, Dr Poulidor, was clad head to toe in protective equipment. She had no idea how the feeble body that she cared for each day resisted the ravages of the global viral pandemic. The scarred and mutilated man before her had every reason to have departed this world long before any number of the young and fit individuals who continued to die around her on the ward. Patients recovering from cancer were known to be highly susceptible to the virus, as were those over 60 years of age, let alone in their late 70s. Something in his DNA made this one was a fighter, that was for sure.

So now the patient was well enough to talk, though his stories were too fantastical to believe. In between fits of coughing, words emerged from his twisted lips in a raspy whisper while his hollow eyes flickered their own story. Rhyme and reason tumbled from him in a mixture of French and English describing trees and nature, while tears of love and loss wet his pillow. She lingered to listen as long as she could before duties called her exhausted attention elsewhere.

2044

༝

LE FIN DE DÉBUT

When death has come for you four times already, you're unlikely to succeed in cheating it a fifth time. Some might say that I was never supposed to live beyond my birthday, let alone find love, enjoy the fulfilment of a career in nature, or achieve entrepreneurial success beyond my wildest dreams. What might I say in return? You might want to wear my skin and maybe you think you could slough it off as easily as the adder that spooked the savage sanglier. Would you watch the love of your life snatched from in front of you, never to return? Perhaps you would trade your sight and all the years afterwards when you could see the wonders of nature, just for that love to be returned.

All I know is that I have lived a life, and I hope that yours brings you the same satisfaction. You must never look back, only forward. There is no end, only another beginning and a life of endless possibilities. Every morning, stretch your wings and sing your heart out.

WOODLORE FOR
YOUNG ASSASSINS

U ntil yesterday, when I bumped into a real Nazi, my only enemy was the bull in the lower field, although there's also the nettles which I keep mistaking for ordinary weeds. Anyway, it was him, I knew it was, that Rudolf Hess. I told Mrs Price and she said it must be. There were two things which meant it was him. He had the biggest eyebrows I've ever seen, and he actually said 'guten morgan' to me (Mrs Price says that was 'good morning' in German, and she told me how to spell it). There were two Welsh soldiers with guns who followed behind his guards. I know they were Welsh because one of them said 'bor-reh dah'. So, there were actually three things which mean it must be him, as no one round here has guards.

I wrote a letter to Mummy yesterday, but I've not told her about Rudolf Hess. Not yet. I thanked her for the yellow gingham dress she sent for my 13th birthday. Mrs Price gave me a knife—it's the best present ever—it says 'Sheffield Steel' and 'Made in England' on the blade, which folds, and it has a real wood handle. Danny Price showed me how to sharpen it, and some ways of whittling a hazel stick. I think Mummy must be very sad about Daddy because she did not mention him in the letter. She reminded me that I have been in Abergavenny for 18 months. She said all the children from my old school have now been evacuated.

I was picking some pretty little red flowers in Pant Skirrid Wood. I've learnt a shortcut and it takes me less than an hour to get there now. Danny told me later it was scarlet pimpernel, just like Sir Percy Blakeney in the Baroness's book. Imagine! I'd finished pressing some of its flowers in my notebook and just stood up after spending a penny, when the Nazi came down the hill and round a bend in the path. I noticed his boots first because their tops were so shiny, although their soles were covered in the wood's red mud. Then the two guards appeared with guns slung over their shoulders. I didn't say anything. I was relieved not to have been caught with my knickers down.

Mummy wrote a funny story in her last letter. She says that they sometimes park a mobile AA battery on the road outside the front gate at home—my real home. Mr Churchill thinks it will fool Hitler into thinking we have twice as many guns. Usually the men knock on the doors, mostly to warn the housewives, but also because they know they'll get a cup of tea. The last time, they forgot to tell anyone in the street, and when they started shooting at the planes, Mummy jumped so much she fell off her chair. Then she looked out of the window and saw Mrs Hargreaves throw a bucket of cold water over the men. She said Mrs Hargreaves was so angry that she was stamping her feet like she was doing a jig.

Sometimes when Mrs Price is milking the cows and Danny is helping, I sneak into his bedroom. It smells funny. Even though he is 14½, I am taller than him. He's like a brother I've never had, but less annoying, sometimes. Last week, I was looking through the books on the shelf above his bed. He must have at least twenty all lined up. Behind 'Swallows and Amazons' I found a book which had been pushed behind the others. It didn't have a dust jacket, just a dark red cloth cover, stained and tattered, but the gold lettering on its spine was clear to read: 'Woodlore for Young Sportsmen' by H Mortimer Batten. The book was published in 1922. My dad would have been ten then. I am copying this bit which describes what's in the book:

> *The life habits of British wild animals, game birds, vermin (real and unreal) and their destruction, angling and habits of fresh water fish, rabbiting and snaring, mole catching, skinning and preserving skins, making leather goods, making your own walking stick, making a toboggan, construction of a permanent home in the woods, and taking care of your puppy.*

I've borrowed the book, but Danny doesn't know. I like it a lot, but it made me wish I had a puppy. I think Mr H Mortimer Batten made a big mistake by not including girls.

Every true sportsman knows that in the natural history of the birds and beasts he pursues lies the chief pleasure of the craft. He does not rejoice so much in the killing of them as in being amidst their haunts, and observing their ways with some definite object to lead him on.

Danny heard me talking to his mother about Rudolf Hess. When we were sweeping the milking parlour together, we hatched a plan to observe RH (that's his code name). When Mrs Price went to Newport, we knew she would be gone all day. We made some bully beef sandwiches and carried some fresh milk with us. First, we walked to Maindiff Court Hospital, and wandered through its bow-shaped gates, and on up to the main building. We thought we might see RH there, as that's where they keep him locked up when he's not allowed to walk in the hills. A nurse asked our business, but we lost our nerve and ran away.

Vermin may be divided into three classes, and as follows: Class 1 - those that are destructive to the interests of all people; Class 2 - those that are destructive on game preserves, but may be even be considered beneficial to farmers; Class 3 - those which normally do no harm, though they are commonly persecuted as vermin on account of the occasional behaviour of individual members of their species.

That makes him Class 1, doesn't it? That's what all Nazis are. But, I think that's unfair to golden eagles, peregrine falcons, and wild cats, all of which Mr H Mortimer Batten says are the worst sort.

Generally speaking, one can quite well leave the destruction of vermin to those whose business it is.

Daddy's business was the destruction of Class 1 vermin, but they killed him instead. That means it's my business now.

Danny and I ran until he got a stitch. Then we walked, eventually climbing all the way to the top of the Skirrid. Danny had a Welsh name for it that I couldn't pronounce: Ysgyryd Fawr. He told me that's how it's spelt, but I think it's code. The second word is code for a new fighting force that I'm going to make when I'm grown up, called the Women's Royal Air Force or WRAF. I've not yet deciphered the first word. I wondered if it might be Welsh code because it has no vowels. Danny thought it could be an Atbash cipher, which I'd never heard of. We looked it up together in another of his books and deciphered that it would mean 'Bhtbibw', so he must be wrong. It makes me laugh when I say it out loud.

Danny says the Skirrid is a holy mountain because there was a great thunderclap when Jesus was born, and it was that which made half the mountain slide down. From the top we could see really far. Danny knew lots of the names of places, and he pointed to the sea in the Bristol Channel, and to the Brecon Beacons and Black Mountains. I wondered if we could see France, where Daddy's body lies somewhere. Danny thought we could see Herefordshire but not France.

It was nosi—the word Danny uses to mean it's getting dark—when we reached Pant Skirrid Wood. We watched two nightjars hunting near the edge of the trees. They looked like giant moths, hunting baby moths. We went down the steep main path, the same one that RH had walked with his guards. Under the trees it was black as coal, and when an owl hooted, it made me a jump. Mr H Mortimer Batten says that tawny owls are undesirable, and Class 2 vermin, but I think they're special because they can hunt vermin in the dark. I was going to show Danny exactly where I had seen RH, but we couldn't see anything. At least he couldn't see where I'd spent my penny. I wish I had eyes like an owl.

We were in the doghouse when we got home. Mrs Price had come back early and created a great kerfuffle when she couldn't find us on the farm. The neighbours had come round to help her search for us. I was sent to bed early without supper, but I didn't mind as I was quite tired. Also, I could read more of Mr H Mortimer Batten in secret.

> *The trap is set so as to intercept the passage of the mole as he works along his tunnel, and generally speaking, burrows that go to and from water yield the best results, as they are in most regular use.*

If I am to bump-off (that's 'zhhzhhrmzgv' in Atbash) RH, then I need to find his regular route. I'm getting really good at sharpening hazel sticks. Danny showed me how to heat their points in the coals which make them harder and sharper. Danny and I have worked out how to make a twitch snare. It's not in Mr H Mortimer Batten's book, but I think I'll include it in the survival manual that I'm going to write to help women of the WRAF who are shot down behind enemy lines. The snare is attached to a big sapling that you bend over to the ground to make a giant spring. The spring is held down with a small carved peg made from a branch crotch, balanced carefully against another peg banged into the ground. We caught our first rabbit with it. It's clever because the fox can't steal your catch, even if you don't check it 'til next morning, which we hadn't.

> *Do not set your snare at the mouth of a burrow, but choose as sheltered a position as possible for it.*

Danny doesn't know about Operation Zhhzhhrmzgv RH. I'm going to call it ZRH from now on. I've got a collection of sharpened and hardened sticks, half-a-dozen wire snares, and loads of cord. I've already stashed them near the scarlet pimpernels. It's a sheltered place, far from the hospital, and there is a perfect sapling ash tree nearby. Danny says ash is the most springy of all the trees. I managed to bend it over, but only by climbing half-way up, then leaning out and falling to the ground with it. The sapling was so springy that my feet didn't quite reach the ground, so I had to let it go. It whipped back so fast that some of its leaves fell off. I landed in a patch of wild onions.

I found a spade in the old henhouse, and I've started digging a pit trap at the target area for Operation ZRH. When it's ready it will hold the sharpened sticks, and over the top I'm going to make a bracken lid. If RH misses the twitch snare, then the pit will get him. Even if he's only injured, the Welsh guards will think he's trying to escape or may be attempting to trap them, so they will shoot him dead for me.

Like Mr H Mortimer Batten says, I'm now going to learn the habits of the vermin. That way I can plan when to launch Operation ZRH. When he's dead, I'll tell Mummy.

> *Finally let me say that though our sympathies are with the nature lover who pleads the preservation of certain birds and beasts by attempting to minimise the harm they do, there is not much to be gained by such generous expression of sentiment.*

Everyone believes me to be a dainty flower, but in real life I'm a ruthless assassin without a single ounce of sentiment for any Nazis. One day they'll know me as the female scarlet pimpernel.

THE SAWYERS:

Or, A Tale of Two Halves

UNDER-DOG

※

I t was an austere room, clad in dark wood panels, made more gloomy by the meagre light entering through the high windows on the dimpsy day.

'I swear by Almighty God that the evidence I shall give shall be the truth, the whole truth, and nothing but the truth.'

'Please state your full name for the record.'

'Billy, sir.'

The judge leaned forward, adjusting his wig. 'Mr Evans, you must state all your given names for the court to hear.'

'William Arthur Evans, m'Lord.'

'You should use the address "Your Honour", Mr Evans.'

'Yes, sir.'

'Mr Evans, my name is Mr Rogers, and I am the Prosecution Barrister. I will be asking you questions relating to the events of March last year. After I have finished, then Mr Starck will ask you further questions on behalf of the defence.'

Billy nodded in affirmation, looking to both barristers in turn.

'Will you tell the court your current age?'

'I was born in 1862.'

'That would make you 17 years old. And what is your occupation?'

'I'm an under-dog, sir.'

'We can see that!' came a shout from above.

The courtroom erupted. Two flat caps fell from the public gallery. A lace handkerchief followed, fluttering slowly to the floor.

'Order! You will refrain—silence! The public will refrain from any such remarks again, or I will have the gallery closed in my court.'

'Thank you, Your Honour,' continued Mr Rogers. 'Would you like to tell the court, Billy, what it is that an under-dog routinely does?'

'I am a sawyer. I work in a saw pit.'

'Would I be right in saying that you stand in a hole some six feet in depth, known as a saw pit, whereupon you operate a two-handled saw by manually guiding it in a linear manner along the bole of a tree?'

Billy looked to the judge. 'I'm sorry sir, I'm not sure . . . My job is to pull the rip saw through the log.'

'Ah, I see,' said Mr Rogers. 'You are merely an engine of sorts. So who is it that guides the saw?'

'That would be him,' answered Billy, pointing to the man leaning forward in the dock. 'He's the top-dog.'

'For the record, Mr Evans, are you referring to your former employer, Mr Ash?'

'Yes, but he weren't my employer, sir. That was Sir Richard from the big house. Mr Ash was the top-dog, my gov'nor.'

'And prior to this tragedy, for how long did you work with Mr Ash?'

'Two years.'

'What would be your opinion of Mr Ash as your governor, your top-dog?'

'He was a hard master, but mostly fair. He made me carry more than my share of heavy loads, and dig out the pit without assistance, on account of my needing to build more strength, or so he always said.'

'Did Mr Ash ever show any cruelty to you, Mr Evans?'

'Only the usual, 'specially when I was new to the job.'

'And, what was that?'

'He would take the stick to me a little if he thought I were lazying around. Oft'times, I would fall asleep in the pit bottom, being too exhausted to climb out to rest, and he would poke me awake quite viciously. One time, I woke to find him above with his breeches undone, letting his stream play over me.'

The court erupted.

'Silence, I will have silence!'

Mr Rogers waited patiently for the outrage to fade. He looked first to the public gallery, then to the judge, and then one-by-one into every pair of juror's eyes, before turning to the young man. 'That can hardly be termed usual Mr Evans, but perhaps you knew of no other. Was there any other treatment you received from your governor that you wish to remark upon?'

'Only that I was bloodied, sir, but that's been the same for all under-dogs before me.'

'What does bloodied mean, Mr Evans?'

'Oft'times, the farm would bring a large beast to be sliced in half before it were sent to the house, but that were only after it's insides had been cleaned and bled, so the butchering was not so bad. But it were a tradition for a new under-dog—Mr Ash always said—to saw in half a piglet tied to the transoms while it were alive. I shall never forget the squealing, and the warm gush of blood and gore. Pardon me, Your Honour!'

Mr Rogers waited for the murmurs of the horrified onlookers to subside, looking in vain to the judge hoping he might intervene again. 'It seems to me, that it would be fair to say, that far from being the 'usual' treatment, your superior was more cruel than fair. And remarkably, this was to his apprentice and co-worker, upon which he relied to get the day's work done. Would that be a reasonable comment Mr Evans?'

'I never saw it that way before sir, but as you mention it, perhaps I knew no other.'

'Yes, I believe that to be so, and it is plain that the jury must agree upon this point.'

Billy stood still, head bowed, and with his hands clasped together in front, as they had been since the start of the proceedings. His fawn woollen waistcoat had the appearance of regular use, its sagging pockets emptied specially for the occasion. The white shirt he wore underneath however, was not only freshly laundered, but newly tailored. The young man's only outward sign of nerves was the constant rotation of a large silver ring on his middle finger.

'I had not expected to hear of such abhorrent acts at this point in the proceedings. I would like to return, if I may, to the saw pit. I think it could be important that you describe its workings in more detail to the jury. Could you do that Mr Evans?'

'Yes sir.'

'Good. Then perhaps you could start with the construction of the saw pit, before describing its workings?'

'It's a basic thing, being a pit some 6 feet in depth and 20 feet long. It allows the under-dog to stand at full height and use one end of the saw while it's ripped through a log. There are two side-strakes, which line the pit sides, and the main headsills at each end. The logs are rolled onto the transom beams and held in place by metal dogs while the two us operate the saw. The saw is the ripping sort, not the cross-cut used for felling, you see because—'

'Thank you, Mr Evans, I think that's sufficient details on the saw. And for you, the under-dog, what is it like to work in the pit?'

'It's hot work, even on a winter's day, on account of the effort. There's a great amount of dust from the saw which you end up standing in, which would reach over the tops of your boots if you've not cleaned the pit enough. I wear a cap and kerchief to keep the sawdust off me, but my eyes are most often quite blind at the end of a working day. But then, my job is to pull the saw, and not seeing is of little consequence except when it interferes with my other duties.'

'I see. Well, Mr Evans, let us now talk about the 26th of March last year, and the fateful events which ensued. Do you remember that day?'

'It was a day much like any other sir, though it started with a thick Scotch mist. We were working near the coppices, where all the faggots had been piled high the day before. There was a coupe of oak felled, ready to be sawn into rafters for an extension to the big house.'

'And did it otherwise continue to be a normal day?'

'No Sir!'

'Please tell the court, Mr Evans, what happened that day in the saw pit on the Grace estate.'

'We had worked hard, cutting four rafters and a square beam, and it was early after the noon when we stopped for a break. Mr Ash had said he would put the pot on the fire for tea. I fell asleep in the pit.'

'It sounds to me, that until this point of the day, it had been quite a typical day's work. Would that be right Mr Evans?'

'Yes sir.'

'And then what happened?'

'I woke to an argument between Mr Ash and Mr Richards. It was unusual for Mr Richards to come to the woods at that time of day, but I knew it were him because of his airy words.'

'And do you know what they were fighting about?'

'Your Honour,' interrupted Mr Starcks, 'I request that Mr Rogers rephrase that question as there was no suggestion of a fight.'

'I agree. Members of the jury, you are to discount the question. Mr Rogers, you will continue.'

'Mr Evans,' continued Mr Rogers, 'do you know what the accused and Mr Richards were arguing about?'

'I do not sir, but I heard Mr Ash tell Mr Richards to "naff off", then what sounded like a fight, as there followed a great deal of grunting and scuffling. Like two boars after a sow, I'd say. Then I heard a loud crack, like when a branch cracks in a beech top on a windy summer's day.'

'And all this time Mr Evans, you did not see this argument, this scuffle?'

'No sir, it was very quick and I had only just woke.'

'What happened next Mr Evans?'

'I do not know sir!'

'I am sorry, of course you do not know, as you were assaulted, weren't you Mr Evans?'

'Yes sir.'

'Will you tell the jury of the events which then unfurled, however distressing they may be for you to recount?'

'I woke up with a cracking headache. I was being poked with his stick by Mr Ash, who was shouting at me to get to work. I opened my eyes and was surprised to find it as black as Newgate's knocker.'

'Are you saying, Mr Evans, that it was night when you woke?'

'It was well past dusk. I could just make out the shadow of Mr Ash standing above me, but I could not see any details on account of my sore eyes at that late stage of the day. I was surprised by the situation, then I felt the gash in my scalp when I rubbed my head. I thought then that I must have been out-cold.'

'Do you mean to say that you had been knocked unconscious?'

'I believed so, yes sir.'

'What happened next Mr Evans?'

'Mr Ash shoved my end of the saw at me and told me we were to make a final cut together. I was quite groggy still but managed to hold the saw in the usual way. It was strangely light work, but very soon I was sodden. I could taste the iron, and I knew it to be blood. My hands kept slipping. Mr Ash shouted at me to finish the ripping, which I did with little fervour. I thought it a cruel trick—now that I was no longer his young apprentice—to have been bloodied again.'

'And what then, Billy?'

'I think I were struck on the head again, for when I woke next, it was nearly the morn. It took me some minutes to come to my senses, as my head was ringing most awful. When I felt the sawdust under my body, I realised then that I was in the pit, and not in my bed.'

'What did you see?'

'I had yet to open my eyes, Mr Rogers, as I was in such a stupor.'

'But presumably, you did open your eyes at some point?'

'Yes sir. I opened them and was not surprised to be looking up and out of the saw pit, through the transoms, to the morning sky. It was very melodious, the dawn chorus being in full song.'

'And what did you see next Mr Evans?'

'I found I were tightly wedged so I looked to one side, and I saw a horror like no other.'

'Yes?'

'It was Mr Richards, sir, or at least half of him. Then I discovered his other half to be on my opposite side. I was the filling in a corpse sandwich.'

TOP-DOG

৯৯

Mr Frederick Ash?'

The priest stood in the doorway, a prayer book in one hand, his broad hat in the other, peering into the gloom. He was unusually tall, and had to stoop as he entered, only to remain doubled-over, holding back his retching as he stumbled down the short flight of stairs.

'By gad sir, this is a hell, and you must be common with it!'

'I am very grateful to you for coming Father.'

'It is the afternoon of the Sabbath, lest you forget.'

A guard entered, carrying a small wooden stool, which he dropped and kicked towards the priest, who had taken no more than two steps further into the cell. An open sewer writhed between priest and prisoner, carrying forth the effluvium of the entire population of Newgate prison.

'No Father, I have been marking all of the 22 days that I have been held here in the bowels of this place.'

'Indeed, I imagine you have little else to keep you occupied.' The priest gathered his black cassock before lowering himself onto the tiny stool, placing his hat carefully upon his mountainous knees. He opened the well-thumbed book and looked across to the man opposite. 'It is the tradition, on the last Sunday before execution, for a priest to visit the prisoner to deliver religious ministrations.'

'Father, I wish to speak with you—'

'Let us pray first, shall we?

'Remember not, Lord, our iniquities, nor the iniquities of our forefathers; neither take thou vengeance of our sins; spare us, good Lord, spare thy people, whom thou hast redeemed with thy most precious blood, and be not angry with us for ever.'

The priest closed the prayer book with a snap. 'You will no doubt wish to repent of your sins. It is common by those faced with the ultimate resignation before God, so that his judgement may be just, and your composure secured for—'

'No father, I do not.'

'You should repent, Mr Ash, so that you may cast yourself with an entire dependence upon the mercies of God, through the merits of our Saviour and Redeemer Jesus Christ.'

'Father, I wish not to offend you, for I am a firm believer, but I desire no more prayers.'

'I think, my son, that you should remember your situation before God, and reach a good temper of mind.'

'I understand that Father, but I wish first to confess to the truth. This will be the truth, not as it was told in court and the papers, but a truth now hidden by a heinous crime. Afterward, then perhaps you may offer your last prayer.'

The prisoner stood, shuffling into the only spot of light in the cell. For the first time the priest had a good look at him; he was considerably relieved to hear the shackles rattling securely for he was gazing upon a giant of a man. The sleeves of his filthy grey tunic bulged tightly round his arms, while his hands, which grasped onto the chains, would easily throttle a boar. Reports of his violent crime in the papers had caused a sensation, and now here he was, face-to-face with a sylvan version of the grim reaper. One cartoon in The Morning Mail had shown him as such: standing with his tree trunk legs astride the pit of hell, his bloodied two-handled ripping saw in one hand, and his terrifying gaze directed into the eyes of the reader.

'Give him strength against all his temptations and heal all his distempers. Break not the bruised reed, nor quench the smoking flax,' invoked the priest.

'Father, do not fear me, for whatever stories you may have read, I am not that man. I am the victim of a cruel injustice, forged by a cunning evil. I could never imagine the evils that I have been accused of, much less act them out with the people I love.'

The priest held his tongue, taken aback by the eloquence of the brute before him.

'I had much respect for my under-dog, Billy Evans, and had watched him grow into a strong young man. I would never have treated as him as he described, nor could I imagine the cruelties of which I have been accused. The pig story ... I raised my own pigs at home for the table, and until then I cared for them as part of my family. I would never act out such horrors.'

'Yet, you have been found guilty my son, of a wicked crime. It is not for me to judge you, but I fail to understand any motive for what, you say, are lies.'

'You may not wish to hear the truth Father, but I already have one foot in Deadman's walk, so I have nothing to lose in telling it. That young man was so clever and devious, and such were the lies he spun, it will be no wonder when he takes upon the stage.

'You see Father, Billy Evans was attempting to bribe Sir Richard Grace. He had caught him in the woods mollying with a man. He wrote him a crude note describing what he had seen, and that he would go to the rozzers with it. He said he had a witness too. The sum of his asking was one thousand pounds!'

'By gads, that's preposterous! Sir Richards was most upstanding, a married man with a fine country estate, and a respected businessman. He would never ... never go mollying—'

'He was very fearful of the prospect of a 10-year imprisonment, and the loss of his reputation.'

'But how do you know all this, I mean on what basis do you—'

'It was me Father, I was Sir Richard's Under-Dog, his bitch. He was my beautiful ... my fortuni lover. He was so handsome. He always wore his long dark ends tied in a ponytail, and I lived for the soft touch of his fambles, the gaze of his sparkling yews. I loved him. And he ... he loved to dominate me.'

The priest was agog, barely concealing his curiosity. 'Was he really, "so", as you say?'

'We would meet regularly in the coppices after dark, enjoying our illicit charver. I know you will think this to be unnatural and sinful, but we wished only to celebrate our love, and to shield his wife from the pain of knowing.'

'If what you say is true, why then did you murder your ... your lover?'

'I did not Father. Imagine instead, if you will, that it was not I who had a fight with Sir Richard, but my wicked accuser. Sir Richard told me that he would offer Billy Evans some money, but not the ridiculous amount he had asked for, and then dismiss him from his employment. I can only imagine that the meeting did not go so well, for when I ... I—'

'Mr Ash, you do not have to continue.'

'On the contrary Father, you must hear me out ... I mean, if you will.' Frederick Ash wiped his eyes on his sleeve and let out a long tremulous sigh.

The priest adjusted his cassock, and closed his prayer book, clasping it tightly against his chest. It offered a small protective shield against the giant sylvan devil.

'Often, I would walk to work in the company of Jeffrey, one of the farm hands, who had a tied cottage next to mine, and so it was that morning. The farm buildings were a little past our saw pit, and he was on his way to them, but still in ear shot, when I discovered the gruesome scene. Hearing my shout, he came running back and was a witness to the scene as I discovered it.

'But no matter Father, all this was said in court, and none was believed. I said only what I saw and had no alibi to preserve me.'

'Yet Mr Ash, I do not understand why you did not share with the court these things you are telling me? You would receive 10 years for unnatural acts, but surely that would be preferable to the ultimate punishment you face, and justice would be served?'

'I could never in public tell the truth about Sir Richard. I would serve my years, yet it would tear his family apart. And so, I have kept my tongue.'

'And what about Billy Evans?' asked the priest.

'Ever since the day he discovered us, he started his accursed plotting. He became unbearable to work with, and most disrespectful. I know now that he was very capable of the crime by himself. Forgive me for the details Father, but by standing on the transoms he could have sawn through my lover's ... his dear soft body easily without the need for an under-dog.'

'And how did he expect to get away with it?'

'He had no need to clean himself after the crime, nor find an alibi, just recline there and wait to be discovered. He would not only get revenge on Sir Richard, but on me too. It was a crime of hatred to our nature and avarice, in equal measure.'

'Now that three Sundays have passed, my son, there is no possibility of changing the course of justice,' stated the priest. 'Do you want me to make a record of your admissions of truth?'

'No, Father. By the grace of God, please protect his family.'

The priest waited, as tears fell freely from the stricken man before him.

'You may perhaps go to the rozzers and mention to them the silver ring which Billy Evans has taken to wearing. A small justice may be done if that despicable man were to be jailed for theft.'

'Dearly beloved, it hath pleased Almighty God, in his justice, to bring you under the sentence and condemnation of the law. You are shortly to suffer death in such a manner, that others, warned by your example, may be the more afraid to offend; and we pray God, that you may make such use of your punishments in this world, that your soul may be saved in the world to come.'

THE FORDING

Astory is like the journey of a great river. It originates at its upland head as a tumbling stream. Along its course, tributaries join, offering embellishment or distraction. Finally, it flows out into the sea at its mouth as a strong and wide current where it shares its waters with those of countless others. For its entire course, the energy of the story is dependent upon sufficient rain falling at the headwaters, interest must come from the character of its telling, and power from the depth of its flow.

Some say that I'm a scribe. I like to think of myself as a magician. Naturally, the magic starts not with me, nor in my pen, but in the head of someone else. The creature will have a memory, thought, or idea which comes first from within their head, then travels out of their brain in their bloodstream, before flowing from their mouths in a series of ticks and clicks, huffs and puffs, whistles and expletives. These noisy expressions are usually accompanied by a great amount of wrinkling of the skin, twisting this way and that on the brow and especially around the corners of the mouth. Even the eyes tell a story, revealing more of the truth than any of the reverberations. When the character is excited, there can be no bounds to the amount of hand gestures, arm waving, even whole-body demonstrations that will accompany these sounds.

This is when the magic begins, and I can weave my spell. My trick is to abduct these thoughts-to-sounds from thin air. It's like chasing the papery seed of an elm as it flutters to ground in a breeze; if you're too slow or clumsy it will hide in the long grass of the riverbank or fall on water only to be swept downstream. My task is to listen and observe, to understand the words and their meaning, and then in a flurry, capture them forever. I must sweep up each sound with my etymologist's net, capturing a ruddy darter resting on a reed, a brimstone rising from a rock, or a purple emperor parading around an oak, and then pin them onto paper. My only tool is not a wand, nor of course a net and pin, but a simple dip pen.

And so it was that I found myself, pen in hand and sitting across from an old woman, at a table in a tavern of dubious quality in middle England. The table, I should add, was the most rustic sort, made from thick planks of elm. Over countless decades its rough sawn surfaces had been expertly filled by hordes of clients using only the finest pig fat, polished smooth with spit and drunken elbow grease. Its dark glossy finish had been lovingly applied with layer upon layer of ale, the last coat of which I discovered still to be tacky. My lowest sheet had stuck fast, and my muse studied me in silence as I peeled the spoiled paper free and fed it to the fire with a curse. The flames signalled their enjoyment with a flare of orange licked with green. I took my time organising my little box of tricks, but my subject seemed more than content with the large ale that I'd furnished her with.

Earlier that morning I'd left my horse at the smiths after it had thrown a shoe, and had decided to fill the day by wandering on foot a little further through the shire which at this time of the year is alight with autumn colours. I descended through the coppery beech woods, past multitudes of sawpits where the top-dogs never ceased their shouting at the under-dogs below them in the wet dust. Each sawpit was surrounded by dozens of chair makers and bodgers, always accompanied by a charcoal maker, and everywhere the children of faggoters were busy collecting sticks for the bread ovens. Beyond the woods lay the great fertile valley of the meandering River Thames, where I soon discovered most of the flat ground is sodden underfoot but must surely provide a rich earth for the farmers. I eventually reached the river itself, and seeing on the other side a tavern, I decided to cross at the ford, marked at its corners like a gateway by two of the largest elm trees I have ever seen. The great city with its spires lay within reach.

The landlady was most accommodating as to my wet stockings and shoes, and after the exchange of a small fee, a young barmaid soon had them hung up to dry alongside a dozen others next to the blazing fire. It was the next moment, as I tip-toed in my bare feet across the sawdust sprinkled copiously upon the flagstones, warm ale in-hand, when the wight had gestured me over. Her ghostly form in the far corner of the dimly-lit room shimmered behind the clouds of smoke which emerged in frequent puffs from her long clay pipe. Observing the black bonnet perched askew her white hair, I assumed her to be a recent widow, yet her toothy grin suggested otherwise. We struck up a lively conversation and it became apparent that I might be able to capture a great many good tales. And so it was, as I say, that I found myself, pen in hand, asking if I might write down some of her words onto paper. She frowned at me but her bright eyes told me that I was in for a treat.

'My pa was an ox-driver, like his pa before him. I never left his side, nor the oxen for that matter, that's how I grew up to be the first woman in the shire to become an ox-driver. Back then I cared for their every need, and always rode behind the broad red withers of Sparrow at the front of the team. I named him as a joke you see. They're always yoked in the same pairs, and we always named the left-hand ox with a "s". Nearest the driver was Snow, and in front of him Sky, then Song. They were yoked with Bunting, Lark, and Thrush. I thought it to be funny to have Sparrow on the left, 'cause I knew everyone would be befuddled that he was named with a "s" but he had the name of a bird and not the character of the bird like the others. I suppose you'll be wondering yourself who Sparrow was yoked with? Well, it was Hawk of course.

'Nothing beats an ox for power, not even the strongest horse of the shire type. With our team of eight, led by Sparrow and Hawk, we could plough the heaviest clays in the valley and pull the greatest cargo from the hills. Oft' times we'd be called upon to extract the biggest sawn beams down from the woods for building in the valley, like the great elm sills for the waterwheel downstream from here. We had the best leather for various parts of the harness, and steam-bent oxbows of elm made to fit precisely the neck of each ox. We used the strongest wood of all for the yokes. I s'pose you'll be wondering what that was, being a town man and all?'

She stopped talking to take a generous swig of ale, draining her tankard. I noticed for the first time that it had two crude ox heads etched as a pair next to its handle. I turned to call the barmaid over but found she was already at my shoulder with a pitcher at the ready.

While the old woman sipped the froth from her freshly-filled tankard, I admitted to her that I had no idea of the likely timber for such a purpose.

'It's none other than the timber from the hornbeam! How else would the tree have found its title?'

My own tankard was being refilled, though I hadn't appreciated it was empty. I nodded, wondering why I hadn't grasped that the clue was in the name. I found myself leaving the main channel, ascending a tributary of my own, thinking about the etymology. I realised that the great oxbow bends of the Thames itself were named after the bent collars used for the oxen.

'... and that's how we found ourselves summoned for a task that no others were up to.'

I jumped from my musings, believing that I'd not missed much, picked up my pen, and once again applied myself to my magic.

'All the houses and other buildings here then, and there weren't many, were made from the timbers of oak and elm, their walls filled with hazel wattle plastered with clay from the riverbed and the marshes. The squire had other ideas. He wanted a stone building, and not just any building either. He had them quarrying limestone from a place near the village of Headington as he said it had to be the finest stone, for the finest buildings, designed for the finest people. That's how that gentleman put it.

'To satisfy the huge quantities of stone to be carried he'd need more than our single heavy wagon and oxen team, but we were given the honour of ferrying the cornerstone for the first of his grand buildings. The day we set out for the stone a heavy river mist lay across the valley, as it oft' does at that time of year. It was only as we laboured up the slopes towards the quarry that the mist cleared, and we enjoyed the rays of the winter sun. At the quarry we had to manoeuvre our team between great blocks of stone and stop precisely beside a landing stage. The quarrymen had a huge oak-framed gin pole and various derricks to lift the massive cornerstone. We'd prepared as best we could, putting extra fat on the axles, but from my vantage on the withers of Sparrow, I looked back fearfully between the curved horns of Song, Sky and Snow to watch as the huge stone was lowered onto the bed of our wagon.

'We'd brought Campion with us, our shire horse, along with our thickest rope, to act as an extra brake as we descended back into the valley. Once safely back on the levels, my youngest brother rode ahead on Campion, and we were relieved that the worst part was over. Our journey became a solstice fête, with families coming out of their houses to watch our slow procession. Many of the small girls threw mistletoe onto the wagon. Some of the silly boys played dares between our wheels. Pa would whip them when he could reach, but they stayed clear of me and Sparrow because he'd the biggest horns and scared most people. They had nothing to fear though, unlike with Hawk; that one looked gentle, yet with him a temper always simmered just below his thick hide.

'By the time we reached the river there was a long procession of people alongside us. The Thames was not running high so we thought little of the crossing as we plodded on, descending the gravel ramp into its waters. We were half-way across when Hawk decided he would slake his thirst. Pa tried to keep him moving, and I spurred on Sparrow. At first he took a few sips while still walking, but then Sparrow lowered his head too and Hawk was able to stop and get a proper drink. The oxen-train and our wagon came to an abrupt halt. The crowd on the bank started to shout, thinking we did not know ourselves the predicament. Pa was hollering and wielding his whip like I'd never seen. Finally, the team decided it would move on. I felt every muscle in Sparrow harden like a rock from that quarry, but we didn't move an inch, let alone a hand. We were truly stuck fast, our wheels sinking ever deeper into the sucking silt of the riverbed. The oxen started to bellow like Jericho might fall.'

I realised she'd stopped talking and was looking at me, apparently waiting for me to make a remark or some such. There was little to say, other than to encourage my storyteller to continue. I asked whether Campion had come to the rescue.

'Ha!' she laughed. 'We realised we were in deep trouble, more trouble than a single horse could fix. A great shout went through the crowd and every farmhand ran straight as an arrow back to their farmsteads to fetch help. By this time, it being the shortest day of the year, the sun was falling rapidly towards the hills and as the air cooled, wisps of fresh river mist had already begun to skate across the ford. I had to work hard to calm the oxen.

'Within the hour, the riverbanks on both sides were lined with people holding rushlights, and some of them made an avenue of lit torches out towards us from the two elms on the far bank. Teams of four or six oxen arrived from every quarter, and each in turn were fixed to our wagon with ropes that together must have measured many furlongs. First with 14, then 18, and even with 22 we could still not be persuaded to move. Only when 34 oxen were harnessed, the largest team ever assembled in all of England, did we feel the sudden lurch and heard a great sucking sound. From the light of my torch I watched the water bubble round Sparrow's legs and cloud black from the silt of the depths. As we got underway the great elm timbers of the wagon groaned, and I swear I even heard the four hornbeam yokes of our team quiver. An excited cheer rang out, echoing across the valley, bouncing back at us as from a thousand ancients hidden in the dark river mist.'

This being the obvious culmination of the story I grasped the moment to beg a moment to excuse myself, my bladder being unaccustomed to the quantity of beer I had consumed. My magician's hand was weary too, having worked miracles to keep pace with the rapidly-flowing story.

⁊⊷

Feeling much relieved, I ducked back through the entrance of the tavern, and made my way towards my corner. Passing the fire, I was pleasantly surprised to find my stockings almost dry, and satisfyingly warm. My relief was short-lived, when I discovered my storyteller to be asleep, though sleep would be too gentle a term, truth be told. Her head was thrust back against the boards on the wall, her mouth ajar with a stream of spittle running down her whiskered chin. Rolling thunder blew rhythmically from her nose.

The high-water mark of the story may have been reached, yet I had too many unanswered questions. What happened to the stone, was the building ever erected, was the ford at the centre of her story the same that I had waded across myself earlier in the day? Leaning across the table, I was bold enough to touch my storyteller on the back of her hand. I recoiled from the coldness of her skin which I can only describe as being like a burn, such was its chill. A deep shiver ran through me, but I braced myself and using my handkercher for protection, I tried again, to no avail. Frustrated, I followed with a shake of her black-laced wrist, finally grasping her by both shoulders and giving her a firm shake. Her head slumped forward onto the table, but not before she muttered, 'Hawk!'

'She'll be 'ere like that 'til the morn,' said a voice behind me. I turned to see the barmaid looking down on me with pity written all over her florid face. 'I s'pose she had you listening to her stories did she, Sir?'

I asked the barmaid what she knew of them.

'Ha, what don't I know of them you mean. Everyone here as heard them more times than there are stars in the heavens. Did she have you believing that she and her oxen brought the first stone for the university?'

My mind stumbled. The old woman had told me about the stone, but not its purpose. I didn't doubt she was an ox-driver, but such a timeline was impossible. The university had been established more than 350 years ago, in the 12th century.

The barmaid read my confusion. 'Don't let it concern you so much, Sir. She's been round these parts as long as anyone can remember, and it seems, well beyond. No one can recall her for being a young girl, even the most ancient of our patrons.'

'Are you telling me that she's not only old, but—' I couldn't bring myself to say it.

'It must be said, Sir, that we don't talk much about it, as it only disturbs the mind. Thinking of it has the habit of making a dam in your head where it stems the flow of sensible thoughts. Some people have gone quite mad with it.'

'I can imagine,' I answered truthfully.

'I s'pose she told you they named the city after her famous fording?'

'But the city's origins are from the time of the Anglo-Saxons!'

'Well Sir, just think about the name of this place.'

I had to confess that I had failed to notice on arrival, being more focussed on the river I carried with me in my sodden clothes.

'Some say this riverbank was the site of the first building of our great city. Fancy, you came in here and didn't notice the name of the tavern?'

'Well, what is it?' I enquired.

'Honestly, Sir. It's "The Ox Ford" of course.'

NATURE-OLOGY

Oh butterfly, must you tax me?
Purple pattern with a wash of white,
Dashing through pools of shade and light,
Nature's angels, spiriting from sight.
That's lepidopterology!

Bird of wonder, you crossed the sea,
Rare passerine, so pleased to perch;
A viewing army, near the church,
Dazzling nature, all focussed to search.
Fellows in ornithology!

Myriad insects, fly to bee,
Much more than carnage smearing our screen,
Or dose of antihistamine;
Pollination for nature's canteen.
Life-giving entomology!

Sharing our genes by some degree,
Four-chambered hearts, on four legs with fur,
Prowling king, or perhaps scared to stir,
Nature's thriving entrepreneur.
The mirror of mammalogy!

That tiny wasp will need a key,
But not its home of ridge and angle;
Apple, artichoke, and spangle,
Nature's galls and alien tangle.
Mutating cecidology!

Final frontier, perhaps a PhD,
A hidden world, right under your feet,
Bejewelling litter, there to greet,
Be wary though, of what you can eat.
Engineering mycology!

Scarce they would be, without the tree;
Neither lepi, orni, or ento,
No mamma, ceci, or myco.
I wonder why so few have come to know,
The science of silvology!

IN PLANE VIEW

I

༜

ANGEL

Despite what those slags on the landing had shouted, Terry knew he wasn't a loser. He could have girls like them any time he wanted, and usually a quick relief with their sort cost less than a 12-pack of premium. They weren't like her, not like his Annie, or Sadie or ... he wasn't quite sure of her name yet, that was something he was still thinking about. Anise—yes, that was a good name—she was a different class to the usual trash on the estate, like several classes above. In fact, he would go as far as saying she was perfect, like his ideal woman; perhaps even an angel.

Terry had found the binoculars in a car boot sale. The glass of one side was cracked and they didn't focus no more, but he still thought they were pretty cool. He'd once looked through a telescope on a seafront somewhere—Eastbourne it could've been—the ones where you put a coin in a slot. It was powerful, but everything looked a bit misty, and just when he spotted some totty worth looking at on the beach, the timer on the sodding thing had run out. While he walked back to the estate from the car boot with his very own pair of binoculars round his neck, it'd made him feel like he was some kind of Victorian explorer, the ones that used to wear those pith helmets. When he came under the shadow of the tower blocks, some kids had teased him, then kicked a football at his back. He'd booted it over the security fence and onto the railway line; that fucking showed 'em.

As long as you didn't look too close up, things weren't blurry at all. The binoculars were a lot better than the seaside telescope, had cost him less to buy than the hire charge, and he could look through them as long as he wanted. There was '8x40' written on the side that wasn't damaged, but he wasn't sure what it meant. Terry had got some paper and a pencil, impressing himself with his maths. Why Leioptico didn't just print '320' on them, he couldn't fathom, like it was some kind of test or something. Unlike the telescope at the beach he didn't have to close his left eye to see 'cos the broken glass made it black on that side anyway.

He'd taken to watching the birds in the tree outside his balcony and had even moved his armchair so he could sit near the window and rest his elbows on it while he looked through the binoculars. They were mostly pigeons or doves or whatever that sat in the branches right at the top of the London plane tree level with his window. Terry had decided he would go to the library and get a book out so he could learn some of their names. That was before he'd discovered Anise.

Terry was watching two of them at it, brazen as fuck, on a bare branch right near the top of the tree. That cock pigeon kept going back for more, like six times Terry counted, and she never complained. Lucky geezer, no wonder he flapped so much. That was when Terry spotted the girl, right behind the two love birds, in the tower block opposite, bouncing up and down in her sports bra. Her flat was one level below his, and she was on some kind of mini-trampoline in her living room. She wore headphones while she wiggled her hips energetically from side to side. Her dark hair was tied up in a ponytail and bounced up and down slightly out of sync with the rest of her heavenly movements. He'd sat transfixed, one hand down the front of his tracks, watching her in awe until she grabbed a towel and disappeared into the back of her flat. Terry made a mental note of the time.

Over the next couple of weeks, Terry got better at predicting when he should settle down in his favourite chair. His heavenly vision gained a name and he soon learnt the rotation of Anise's fitness outfits. His favourite was Anise's salmon pink sports bra because he could see more details. On one of the pink days he thought he'd died and gone to heaven when, after a particularly vigorous session, Anise had stripped off her top. He'd watched in awe as she towelled the sweat from between and under her tight breasts. Only when she disappeared out back did he realise he'd drooled down the front of his t-shirt.

That was just a couple of days ago, and today while he waited in anticipation, he realised that something was wrong. At first, he thought the binoculars were dirty so he cleaned them on his t-shirt, but it made no difference. Terry's initial anger at his own stupidity turned into a rage when he realised the light green smudges which partially obscured his view of Anise's flat were not dirt, but the emerging leaves of the plane tree which grew between them. It were fucking spring weren't it? He felt like someone had kicked him in the guts as he caught brief glimpses of Anise working out between the dancing green; and it was a pink day too.

Over the next five days, Anise was stolen from him completely by the tree, but for several more days Terry couldn't shake the habit of settling down in his chair at the allotted time. All he could see now was a wall of light green, and the occasional pigeon pecking at stuff. He'd thought about trying to climb the tree with a saw to do some pruning, but it was nearly as tall as his eighth-floor flat, and anyway when he'd gone to look carefully at its trunk—something he'd never really done before—he realised he wouldn't even manage to haul himself onto its first branches which were above his head height.

Finally, after several weeks moping about his flat, Terry began to look more positively on the situation. It was early summer now, but the tree would lose its leaves in five months or so. That gave him time to plan.

II

※

SMOKE

Terry was so motivated, he'd quit smoking. Ever since that damn tree had ruined his fun, he'd been putting the money he'd saved away in a tin. He was impressed with his own determination, and most of all in how he'd gone about researching his options in three different camera shops. The geezer at the first he tried had suggested he spend £500; Terry hadn't been back to that one. The other two shops both stocked a more affordable model, and in the store on Tottenham South Road he'd managed to talk the assistant round to reducing it by another ten quid to £89.99. He was right chuffed until the little squirt had told him, almost like it was an afterthought, that it was so powerful he would need a tripod. That set him back another £39.99 and cleaned him out. That week he'd had to go halves on the lager.

He was so organised that the leaves were still on the stupid tree—although he was sure they looked tired—when he set up the scope and tripod in his flat. It was September and he couldn't remember another time he'd ever thought about the seasons so much. That bloke in the shop had been right about the tripod; even the smallest wobble made it impossible to see what you were looking at, the scope was that powerful. He set up the tripod between his chair and the window pointing the way it should, but it made everything on the tree so big he couldn't even work out which bit he was looking at. Just a whole bunch of green leaves with yellow on their margins. So he aimed the spotting scope to the side, towards the kids' playground and the skateboard ramps in the rec beyond the two tower blocks. Terry couldn't believe how good it was. He could read, not only the graffiti scrawled on the concrete walls, but even the petty messages scratched into the colourful plastic-coated bars on the top of the climbing frame. When he panned over to the same bench he used to sit on to take fresh air while he had a smoke, he watched two young mums talking, like they do. He could read the headline on the copy of the paper resting on the pretty knee of the nearest of the two, even from 200m away. Awesome!

He'd noticed some leaves on the pavements over the last week, and they looked the same as from the tree outside his block. It wouldn't be long now, and he could hardly think about anything else. He was still not smoking and still saving. Terry had discovered on the internet that for another £150 he could get a special adapter for the scope that meant he could record video with his phone. He couldn't afford it yet, but hopefully in a couple of months, and may be sooner if he cut back on the lager, although weirdly he found that harder than quitting smoking. It'd be worth it though because he could rewatch the best bits whenever he needed to.

That damn tree did a more enticing striptease than any of the tarts in the club on Princess Road, like the slowest reveal ever. Day by day, as more green faded to yellow, the shape of the tower block opposite slowly became visible, even though that tease kept Anise's window covered to the very last, like it knew it was the climax of its final dance. Then, after the first storm of the autumn blew through, Terry's day finally came.

Every penny that he'd scrimped and saved had been well-spent, and every frustrating month, week, day, and minute, worth the wait. Instead of the shaky view of the beautiful figure of Anise, now he could see the colour and style of her earrings, the logo on her sports bra, the sweat on her brow. He loved how her lips parted as she rested her elbows on the windowsill after a set of hard reps, and he was hypnotised by the mole rising and falling on the left breast of her heaving chest. For two incredible weeks Terry was in heaven. He barely noticed the days closing in, nor that his muse had started to turn on the light in her room before each session. So it was a surprise when, half-way through her usual 45-minute regime, she reached over and dropped the blind over the window. It took a huge effort to control his rage. He nearly kicked the tripod over as he paced up and down, thumping the side of his head until his knuckles bled.

For the next few days Anise began each workout with the blinds undrawn, but every time she closed them before she reached the end of her session. That meant he missed the moment when she towelled herself down and sometimes stripped before going to the shower. And then, one terrible day, he was blind from the start of the session and could barely enjoy her vague shadow dancing on the fabric of the closed blinds. Fucking winter.

III

❧

SLEUTH

Terry knew that he'd have months to wait and had tried not to be idle. His saving plan was not going well and that meant he wouldn't be able to enjoy Anise when nature next hid her from view. He was pissed with himself about that.

He was well impressed with his sleuthing skills though, like he was a right Sherlock; the one who wore that weird hat with the ear flaps and smoked a bent pipe. One afternoon he'd watched Anise packing her bags, and really early the next morning—he wasn't even sure why he was awake at that time—he noticed that all the lights were on in her flat. She was going away, maybe a flight somewhere. No one packs and gets up that early unless they're going to the airport.

Terry knew that Anise was on the seventh floor, so he'd made a fake package addressed to Mrs Smith in flat 71B, so if he was challenged by one of the Neighbourhood Watch busy bodies in the foreign tower, he'd have an excuse to be wandering round. The next day he realised too late that it wasn't such a good idea to climb the concrete stairs instead of taking the lift. He wasn't sure why he did it, other than because spies and shit in movies always took the stairs. He was exhausted by the time he'd reached the landing on the fourth floor. He never took the stairs to his flat; stupid fucker. Everything in the block was exactly the same as his, but then it wasn't. The stairwell had the same stink of piss, yet the doors were different colours and the graffiti strangely unfamiliar. When he reached the seventh floor it took him a while recover and to orientate himself before he realised that everything was a mirror image of his block. Through the landing window he recognised the plane tree from its size, though it looked very different from its other side, and beyond that, lay his tower block, his flat, his window. The tree strangely comforted him as he walked towards Anise's door. He'd heard the saying before, but before that moment he'd never appreciated what it meant to have your heart in your mouth.

Now that he stood in front of her bright yellow door, clutching the dummy parcel in his sweaty palm, he realised his plan was incomplete. He glanced at a card with the name 'King' slotted in below the bell push. It smelled good standing there, he was sure of that, just the hint of Anise. Just a few steps away would be her wardrobe, her pretty sports bras lined up neatly on hangers. He had a sudden realisation that the door might open at any moment, that someone might be in, even if Anise was away. It was a premonition because the thought was in his mind when one of the lifts pinged and its doors opened behind him. He turned round in horror to see a figure striding towards him. 'You lost or something?' asked the young woman.

Anise was so much in his mind that it took Terry a moment to realise that it wasn't her speaking to him. The woman was of similar age and height, and looked eerily like Anise, but nowhere near as pretty. He opened his mouth, but only managed to mutter something about being on the wrong floor, before running for the still-open lift doors. As they closed behind, he turned to see the woman staring at him through the scratched and graffitied glass. He was cross at himself for panicking, but most of all for not thinking of what actual words he might say in case he was challenged. He should have worn a disguise too, or at least a cap or something; that was stupid.

Terry realised that he was pretty low after the experience because he'd started to drink more. Anise was definitely away. Occasionally in an evening, the lights came on in her flat and someone moved about behind the blinds, but he knew it wasn't her. He'd put a sheet over the scope, not just to protect it from dust, but because it stopped reminding him of how cruel life can be. He'd also started smoking again and his savings were going down rather than up, which only made him feel worse, but he couldn't do anything about it.

One miserable wet day, as he made his way back from the 24/7 store carrying a crate of lager and more smokes, he'd just reached the rec and the point where the tower he called home came into view, when he spotted a white van parked next to his plane tree. It had a flashing orange light on its roof next to an extending lift. Two figures brightly clad in fluorescent overalls and white hard hats were busy stringing hazard tape round his tree and erecting warning signs on the little green between the two blocks.

By the time he reached the activity, Terry had decided that he'd investigate with some clever questions, just like Sherlock. 'Hey mate,' Terry said to the one with his back to him as he reached for something in the back of the van. He nearly dropped his lager when the figure turned round and dazzled him with a pretty smile framed by painted lips. The woman swept a lock of blond hair under the peak of her helmet, 'Yes love?' Every word he planned to say escaped him. He felt himself blush, but finally managed to say, 'what're you doing?' There was no way he was going to ask what the fuck she was on about with her answer about pollarding cherry pickers and what have you. He nodded, satisfied at least to know they were going to do something with his tree, before hurrying home.

He didn't dare use the spotting scope as they might see him from their platform while they worked. It hovered not far below his window and his trusty old binoculars were easier to use anyway because the target moved around quite fast. The female tree cutter was working from the elevated platform with a small chainsaw, her companion on the ground working the ropes from below. Bit by bit, she was cutting the branches away, like giving his tree a severe haircut. He enjoyed watching the treedresser at work, even though she was made androgynous by her work overalls. What really excited him though was the dawning realisation that she was cutting so much off the tree that next spring and summer he'd be able to watch Anise without interruption. Life had just got seriously better. He would so quit smoking again and buy that camera mount.

It was amazing what you could get from an online auction. He'd managed to bid successfully for a 28-piece professional lock-picking set. It even came with a padlock to practise on. It took him a week before he could release the padlock with his eyes closed. Then he moved onto the lock on his own flat door. It'd shocked him how easy it was, but then again it was good news, as it was probably the same type as Anise would have on her door as no-one bothered to change them because you needed permission from the landlord. He became super fired-up about his new spy skills. One night, he couldn't resist breaking into the janitor's locked cupboard and helping himself to some loo roll; another couple of quid saved towards his camera adapter. He became so practised that he never used the real key to his door anymore, and he could now enter his flat almost as quickly with the pick.

Terry had also been back to the seventh floor of the sister tower, not once, but now on a daily basis. Some of the residents even said hello like he was one of them. He wasn't sure this was a good thing, as he thought a good spy should not be easily recognised, but then it meant that he wasn't challenged anymore. He'd worked out the best route, and even knew that the righthand lift was a few seconds faster than the left. His best time was 4 minutes 59 seconds, door to door, and never more than 5 minutes 30 seconds.

Anise had better return soon.

IV

୬୧

Ecstasy

She was back; Anise had arrived late the previous night. It was early April and the leaves were emerging on the plane tree now far below his line of sight. He cleaned the scope optics and settled down with a lager to watch her window as soon as it was light. A pink dawn leant an eerie glow to the facade of her block, and Terry was nearly through his second tinny when she first appeared.

His mobile was fully charged and already mounted on the scope thanks to the adaptor he'd finally purchased a few weeks before. He'd discovered that it worked really well after making a few test runs, filming girls in the rec and some dummy recordings of Anise's empty flat. And now his girl was back home and she looked fantastic, like she'd had lots of winter sun. Everything was in place; life couldn't get any better than this. It wasn't her usual exercise time, but he started recording anyway.

His mouthful of lager showered all over his tracks when he spied a second figure in the flat. Anise had come into view wearing his favourite pink top and Terry had watched her busily setting up the gym equipment in their usual positions. She'd come towards the window and placed her water bottle on the sill when the well-built naked torso of a male materialised behind her from the shadows of the room. The figure pushed her face up against the window and a large black hand came from behind to cup her left breast, hiding her delicious mole from Terry's view. Her head bent back as the man pulled her dark ponytail. Anise reached behind with both hands, pulling him towards her, tugging down her leggings to expose that delicious tight arse for him.

Terry couldn't take his eye off Anise. He studied her closely as her face began to flush, watching how her lips slowly parted, her eyes screwed shut, and finally when her eyelids began to flutter. Her perfect breasts pulsated on the sill, and at the end of her tightly-muscled outstretched arms, her slender fingers curled and uncurled in time to hidden waves of ecstasy.

V

Disco

Terry had the worst headache ever, and it took several minutes before he could open his eyes. When he finally managed to squint into the room, he was surprised that it was almost dark, and the glow of the muted tv pulsed in time to his throbbing head. He didn't remember opening the window, which was something he rarely, if ever did, because it was always too noisy. Some fucking pigeon was cooing in the skeleton of the plane tree below but was soon masked by a jet making its final approach to the international airport. As the roar faded, he heard another sound; his washing machine was running. It wasn't Saturday and he had no recollection of doing any laundry.

He realised that he was staring at his hands, turning them over repeatedly as if there was a new pair on the end of his arms. What the hell? He was totally naked. Something was going on, and whatever it was, he didn't like it. He tried to recall how the day had gone, looking down at the side of his chair for the tell-tale pile of empty tinnies after an all-day session, but there were only two on the floor. Terry began to shake. Then he noticed blue disco lights flashing on the walls of the tower block opposite and sparkling blue twinkles in the pane of his open window.

As he made to stand, his legs almost gave way. He put his arms out to steady himself and they ached like hell. Terry reached the open window and within seconds realised that he'd been mistaken. There were four separate police cars stopped at the entrance to the other tower. Holy shit, something serious was going down! He staggered to the bedroom and pulled on his robe, before cursing while he searched for the tv remote in the chaos of the main room. Fucking cushions.

Finally. His shaking fingers pressed 1 and 9 for the news channel and fumbled for the unmute button.

News of Brexit and FTSE figures scrolled past in the bottom of the screen, but the main screen featured a scene of blue flashes lighting up a pair of familiar concrete towers. 'There's breaking news tonight, here at the Ophelia Towers,' said a starkly-lit female reporter wrapped in a ridiculously unwrinkled mac, 'of a double murder.' The views switched from close-ups of hastily erected barrier tape with the word 'police' repeated along its length, to residents leaning out of their windows above. 'So far police have not issued a formal statement, but I spoke with one resident tonight who supported the rumour that one of the victims was a talented Olympic hopeful.'

Behind the reporter, the amputated limbs of the plane tree flickered blue. Somewhere beyond its truncated crown, and behind one of the brightly-lit windows of the looming south tower, Terry realised that he was an invisible extra starring in the live tv drama.

He went over to the window and looked across to the other tower and Anise's flat. All the lights were on, but the blinds fully drawn, as they were for most of the apartments. Something was unsettling him, and it wasn't the news of another so-called tragedy. Stabbings were rarely news these days, with so many petty drug wars and gangs on the streets, so it was surprising that the press were headlining the story. He watched the rolling news for another hour, but nothing original was said, just endless filler shots and reworded versions of news already shared. Some of the residents came forward to be interviewed. He recognised one as a young mum he liked to watch supervising her kids in the rec. She said she was scared for them.

It was all too much for Terry and he felt totally exhausted. He turned in early and slept a fitful night of vivid dreams.

VI

⁓

Shrine

It was late morning when Terry finally managed to leave the flat. His mind still felt fuggy and his limbs ached almost as much as his head. As he opened the entrance door of the south tower his eyes were immediately drawn to the collection of gaudy bouquets placed at the base of the plane tree. His head throbbed so much he daren't bend down to view the cards on the ground, but he read several pinned to the tree's trunk. The hand-drawn messages said things like 'Laura RIP' or 'We love you Laura' alongside crudely-drawn pink hearts and snowflakes. Even while he was there, two people added more bunches of flowers and messages to the makeshift shrine.

It was a struggle, but he made it to the 24/7 where he picked up some pills for his head, a four-pack of lager, and a copy of the local rag. On the return leg he made it as far as his smoking bench before he had to pause. He wished he'd bought some water so he could have taken the pills straight away. With difficulty he sat down on the bench and breathed slowly through his nose, looking across to the two towers, the lopped plane tree, and the small crowd gathered around its base. He opened up the back of the paper. He liked to have a flutter each morning and started scanning through the day's races listed under his favourite bookies. Decision made: Kempton Park, 3.15pm, Legal Eyes, 4/1F. Terry reached for his mobile to place the bet, but it wasn't in his favoured pocket, nor in any of his others. Where's the fucking thing? He flipped the paper over in frustration.

'Olympic Hopeful Brutally Murdered' read the headline, and underneath it a quarter-page photo of his Anise smiled cheerfully back at him. He retched, then retched again and again, until his insides hammered against his ribs. A young mum walking by with a push chair gave him a wide birth, shaking her head in disgust as she carried on still talking into her phone.

Terry picked up the paper again, his hands trembling, and began to read.

> *Laura King, a 19-year-old athlete and Olympic hopeful, was found dead late yesterday afternoon at her flat in south London. Police have released a short statement to confirm that two bodies were discovered by a sister of one of victims.*
> *Statements given to this reporter by local residents speak of blood coating the walls of the flat, with further traces seen on the landing and lift doors. Unconfirmed rumours are circulating of sightings of a suspicious character in the vicinity over recent weeks. Police have urged residents to report any information to them and not to take any direct action.*
> *Laura had just returned from the Austrian Alps where she had been training with the British team for the forthcoming Winter Games. Her daring signature 'back-to-back 1080' in the snowboarding half-pipe competition was ...*

Terry's stomach lurched again but was hideously empty. The bile stung the back of his throat, and he wished again that he had some water.

At that moment the image of his phone came into his mind. That's where it was, attached to his scope back at the flat. He'd left it there, recording ... recording Anise and ...

VI

❧

HEARTS

Terry had no idea how he made it back to his flat. He paused briefly among the gathering crowd at the base of the plane tree and brushed away the tears so no one would notice, but felt suspicious eyes staring at him. He had a dark stain down the front of his tracks and he stank like shit, and felt like shit. He left a tin of lager among the flowers and, head down, hurried to the entrance of the south tower.

Back in the flat, he popped a couple of pills and gulped down some water from the tap, before wetting his fingers and running them through his matted hair. He pulled off his tracks before collapsing into his favourite chair and opening a tinny to wash away the cloying taste. His eyes rested on the scope with the fancy camera mount he'd saved so long for, and in its grasp, his mobile phone. Its battery would be flat by now, but it could wait.

When he woke it was still light outside. His body ached but his head felt better. Terry stood up and looked through the window. Far below, the pile of flowers and message cards had spread wider than the width of the tree's leafy canopy. Pink shiny heart balloons jostled for attention among hand-drawn cards. A policewoman stood near the entrance to the north tower checking people entering, and a two-man tv crew roamed the scene hunting for stories. Anise's blinds were still drawn. Terry picked up his trusty binoculars and scanned the windows opposite. On the landing of the seventh floor there was blue and white tape across the lift doors, and someone clad head-to-toe in a white suit was on their knees cleaning something, or studying it.

Terry plugged his mobile into its charger, and while the stupid wheel on its screen went round and round, he cracked open another tinny.

When he'd bought the camera mount, he'd also asked for a cable so he could stream the contents of his phone to the tv. He'd tried it once and it worked a treat. Finally, the phone came to life and he connected it up to the tv while it continued charging.

It was like he was looking live through the scope ... no, it was better. The image was larger and he would be able to watch scenes again and again. Terry watched the unmoving image of Anise's empty room, knowing what would come next. He watched her appear and move about the flat in her pink top, busy setting up the gym equipment. The best bit was to come, the moment when Anise became animal, and when it arrived he paused play so he could relieve himself. Strangely he couldn't remember what happened next. He relaxed into the chair and watched in fascination as the couple started another passionate session against the window, in fact, he enjoyed it for another four minutes 59 seconds.

VI

୬ଡ଼

SMILE

It was like an old silent horror movie, but without the piano track and the subtitles. One minute the lucky fucker looked ready to finish, and the next, his throat opened up like a giant mouth and spewed blood over the girl's back. Anise screamed silently, whipping her head round so fast that her ponytail lashed the window pane. She straightened up and turned round with her hands up, defending herself frantically as the knife came at her again and again.

Terry frantically struggled to pause play with his trembling fingers.

He hurried over to his main phone and dialled 999.

'Emergency, what service do you require? Fire, police, or ambulance?'

'It's the murder, I've just seen the murder!'

'Sorry sir, can you confirm that you've just witnessed a murder?' asked a calm female voice.

'Yes … I mean, no,' Terry stammered, 'I mean it's not just happened, I've filmed it.'

'You've captured a murder on your camera. What's your name sir?'

'Terry.'

'Where are you now Terry?'

'I'm in my flat. 81F in the south tower at Ophelia.'

There was a brief pause. 'OK Terry, the police are already on their way to you, can you stay on the line?'

'Yes, if you want.'

'Can you do something for me Terry?' asked the soothing voice. 'Can you tell me when you see the officers' car arrive?'

'Yes, I can do that,' answered Terry, moving to the window. He craned his neck to look from the base of the plane tree and out towards the road entrance. Sure enough, within a couple of minutes he could hear a distant siren and shortly after a silver car with a blue flashing light pulled to a halt below his tower. 'They're here.'

'That's good, Terry. Now I want you to do something else. Will you stay on the phone, but open your door?'

'Okay,' he answered, but as Terry walked to the door a cold sweat overcame him. What if they think that I've been spying on people, on Anise? Shit, they'll think I had something to do with this! He looked from the scope poised next to the window, and over to the tv which remained frozen at the moment the knife had entered Anise's soft belly. Panic swept through his mind, he had to think clearly.

'Terry, have you done that for me? Have you unlocked the door?'

'Shut up will you, just give us a minute to … I've got to think a minute!'

'Terry,' came the voice, firm now, like his Mum's always was before she beat him.

'I'm sorry, look I didn't mean it. I was joking that's all ...' He cut the call. Maybe they wouldn't come up now, they'd be called back to base. Terry looked nervously out of the window. The unmarked police car was still there. He should hide his scope, that's what he ...

The door to the flat burst open and two armed police entered, shouting for him to get on the ground. Terry hesitated, but not for long. He was bundled to the floor and while one of them pinned him down with his knee, the other cuffed his hands behind his back.

Terry decided that he shouldn't say anything in front of the two police thugs, so he sat in silence while they waited together for the assistance to arrive that they'd requested over their radio. They had asked him if he wanted to sit in his chair and he'd nodded. One stood behind him as the other walked carefully round the flat. He'd seen the two exchange a glance, looking from the scope to the tv and back again. The restless one moved over to the window and looked thoughtfully across to the tower opposite.

After too long, far too fucking long, a woman entered his flat, like she owned it. She wore a grey trouser suit and a police identity card round her neck on a blue lanyard. She looked like a Russian shot putter. Terry shivered.

'Hello, Terry isn't it? Look, don't be scared, I'm sure we can clear this all up. Rob would you take the cuffs off him? My name is Detective Spanica.'

'Thanks,' replied Terry as the cuffs came off. He rubbed his wrists. 'Look, I phoned because ... well, I saw the murder on a film I made. I didn't mean nothing by it. I did the right thing telling you didn't I?'

'Yes, you did Terry,' answered the woman, who maybe was more kind than she looked. 'Can you show us this film?'

'It's on my mobile and on the—' The tv displayed a screensaver of its brandname, which bounced randomly across the screen. Terry went to move towards it.

The detective pushed him firmly back into the chair. 'No ... sorry Terry, let us do that.' She held up the remote. 'Which button is it?'

Terry told her and watched as the tv came to life. The final scene returned, still paused at the fatal moment. The detective gasped. 'Did you take this with that?' she asked, pointing towards the scope.

Terry nodded.

'That's a powerful rig you've got there. Keen on birdwatching are you?'

Terry studied her trousered legs. She had a double crease in them and the knees had worn a little.

'Can you tell me how I play the film?' she asked.

He complied and the stillness of the horrific scene erupted suddenly into silent violence. Anise doubled over in front of a shadowed figure, her pale arse towards the camera. The figure wore a blood-splattered tracksuit and a baseball cap hid his face as he watched his victim slump to the floor. He clutched a long kitchen knife in a bloodied hand and its blade glinted as he stepped round the body and moved towards the window. He raised his head to look out, not just at the view beyond the window, but directly into the camera, like he knew it was there. On the tv screen a smile broke out across Terry's blood-splattered face. In the flat, the live version of Terry howled in anguish.

THE COOPER'S TALE

T hanks to the great oak barrel which he'd clung to, the shipwrecked sailor survived the terrible storm that destroyed his frigate. He was the only one among 200 crew to make it alive to a tiny desert island in the eye of the vast ocean. He had since lost track of time but owed his life to the barrel for a second time when he discovered that it contained drinking water. One morning, maybe weeks but possibly months later, the lonely sailor was excited to discover another barrel washed up on his solitary sandy beach. It was heavy and he struggled to roll it above the high-water mark. He only realised what was inside when it rolled away from him and dropped into a small hollow with a bump. A shout of "ow!" had startled him and he worked quickly to prise off its header. He was amazed to find a young woman inside. She was delighted to see daylight, to breathe fresh air, and to meet not only another human being but a man at that. Once their joyful greetings were over, she asked, "would you like some roast chicken?" Naturally the sailor was amazed and excited, because for a long time he'd eaten only raw fish. When they'd finished their delicious meal, she reached deep inside the barrel and brought out two glasses of beer. The sailor couldn't believe his luck. As the two enjoyed their tipple they shared their incredible survival stories. As the sun began to dip below the horizon the young woman asked, "would you like to play with me, it's been a long time since I've had good company?" The sailor thought he'd died and gone to heaven. "What instruments did you bring?" he asked, looking inside the barrel.'

Inside the workshop the older of the two men stopped speaking and looked expectantly at his companion. He could hear a robin in full song just beyond the cracked windowpane, but inside it was deathly quiet. Tommy raised his bushy eyebrows and cocked his head towards his young companion.

'I'm not sure Tommy, was that a joke or some'ing?'

'Really? Here's another then. Knock knock.'

'Tommy, do we 'ave to do this?'

The old man's smile faded, and he turned away.

'Alright, alright ... who's there?'

'A cooper,' said the old man, looking over his shoulder with a grin.

'A cooper who?'

'A coo, purr, hoo ... woof, miaow, moo ... neigh, howl, coo ... cockadoodle—'

'Stop, stop! On my grave Tommy, your jokes ain't the slightest bit funny. If you didn't know us, you'd never know my pearly whites disappeared in a pub brawl. Like, where's my grin? If there ain't a grin, then you've no hope of a laugh now 'ave you?'

The old man slowly stroked his beard its full length down to his chest, then adjusted his grubby shoulder braces. He let out a slow sigh, then as if remembering something asked, 'tell me this, my young friend, why did the cooper eat his lunch on a barrel?'

'I don't know, Tommy.'

'Cos he was staving hungry!'

''onest Tommy, give up, will you? Everyone knows you are a master cooper and that your barrels are the finest in all of Westonberg, but making laughter just ain't your thing.'

'A man walks into a bar—'

'Enough!'

'... and he looks at the beer pumps along the bar top, the fancy fruit ciders and the like, and he's disappointed until he spots a whiskey barrel on its side behind the bar. It's well-made, probably ex-French brandy. It has the drink's age and fancy logo branded in the oak of its fine-figured header. "Excuse me," says the man, "I'd like a double." Without warning the barman turns round, reaches under the bar, and shoots him with a shotgun. "Another satisfied customer," chuckles the barman.'

'What the—'

'There, you liked that.'

'What the hell makes you think that Tommy?'

'Your lips twitched.'

'I was wincing.'

'Darn me,' said the cooper, lifting his tweed flatcap and wiping his forehead with a handkerchief lifted from his shirt pocket. 'Well, in my mind it was the start of a grin.'

In one corner of the workshop, the embers from small oak offcuts glowed in a raised fire bed. Most of the light in the cluttered space came through a dusty window, half of which was shielded by trailing ivy curtains. A tendril of the pioneering plant had reached through a sharp triangular break in the glass and unbelievably seemed to consider it was worth exploring inside. A haphazard collection of cobwebbed lightbulbs lent a soft glow to the shadows, but the two men loitered in a shaft of sunlight which streamed through the little window. The cooper perched on his shave-horse, absentmindedly running his thumb across the razor-sharp edge of a curved drawknife which rested on the leather apron covering his lap. His companion stood with his back to the window, arms folded like he didn't want to touch anything which might be dusty, let alone dangerous.

Between them stood a large oak barrel with freshly shaved sides and shining steel hoops. Its inside had been recently toasted and the aroma of burnt oak filled the workshop. A curious monogram had been branded on the barrel's header, partially obscured by a few oak shavings and a scrap of worn paper filled edge-to-edge with italic writing, most likely flourished with the wide carpenter's pencil lying next to it. Against the rim a large cork stopper lay on its side, waiting expectantly to fill the hole which the cooper had evidently drilled in readiness along the mid-line of the barrel's bilge.

'Why won't you tell me what this is all about?' asked the young man, his eyes leaving the barrel to gaze down at the man next to him.

'I was sworn not to tell a living soul. I was told it was a most serious matter.'

'How come?'

'The young lady made it very clear that I was not to divulge anything about our conversation to anyone, let alone what she'd asked me to make—darn it, now see, you've got me saying things I shouldn't.'

'You can tell us Tommy, we're like family almost ain't we?'

'That may be, but I shouldn't say more.' The cooper lowered his voice. 'All I know is I've been coopering all my life and I've never had anyone ask for a barrel for that reason.'

'So, you're making a barrel then, but what's with the obsession in jokes?'

The cooper stared at him a moment before the hint of a grin spread between his silver whiskers. 'You know I'm not a young man anymore and I've been thinking that I should make a bucket list before I pass. I mean, I reckon it's time I branched out and tried my hand at something new. I want to make a pail, tub, cask, pot, scuttle, pitcher, butter churn, keg, bowl ...'

'That's better than the others, but it don't deserve more praise than that.'

'There you go, we're getting there.'

The young man shook his head. 'I'll put this in language you understand old man. How many planks go into one of these big barrels?' he asked pointing across to the drum of barrels stacked next to the large barn doors.'

'You mean staves, not planks. Thirty-one, give or take. I like French oak best as they grow them even and slow, so th—'

'Right, 31. So you might try 31 jokes on me, and everyone can be about barrels for all I care, but I'm telling you straight, jokes just ain't your thing. Maybe the grain's all wrong in you or some'ing, d'you get my meaning?'

'Did you hear about the woman who went over Niagara Falls in a barrel last year? She barrel-y made it.'

'I can't stand any more Tommy, 'onest I can't.'

'Will you not help me?'

The young man, who had buried his face in his hands, raised his eyes at the slight tremor in the old man's voice. 'I can't help you if you won't tell me what this is all about now can I?'

The cooper took his hanky from his top pocket again and as he dabbed his forehead, motes of sawdust floated and eddied in the shaft of sunlight. 'You have the best laugh I've ever heard, and I've thought through everyone I know. Old Mick had a great one, and he would have helped bless his soul, but among the living I can't think that I know a better one than yours.'

'And why would you be wanting a laugh like mine?'

'I ... I can't say, honestly I've been sworn not to.'

'Tell me about this barrel then. What's so special 'bout it?'

'I don't know—'

'You can tell me 'bout your coopering can't you, if not the laughing thing?'

The cooper looked down at his hands, and if realising for the first time that he held the drawknife, he turned it over to inspect it from every angle. He rested a hand onto the barrel between them. 'It's the best I've ever made, that I can say.'

'And why's that?'

'I've never had a wet barrel leak any wine, beer, or spirit, and neither has a dry one allowed its flour, dried rosebuds, or gunpowder to escape. None of my white barrels have failed the butteries or milk parlours.'

'Everyone in Westonberg knows that Tommy, like I said, didn't I?'

'You did, and I suppose that's why she sought me out.'

'And what did she want from you?'

'"The best barrel you've ever made," is exactly as she put it. And this is it.'

'Why does it feel we're going round in hoops Tommy?'

'What I can say is that it's been made, not for anything wet, or dry, or even any dairy, but something altogether different,' said the craftsman, his eyes darting to the open workshop door.

'You're making me think back to my school days.'

'They weren't so long ago were they?'

'Thanks, old man! So, there's liquid matter, solid matter, and a third kind ... that's it, gas. Now, wait a minute Tommy, you ain't putting no poison in there are you, because if you are you'll—'

'No, nothing of that sort.'

The young man started to pace up and down in the cramped space between the cooper on his shave horse, the barrel, and the old brick wall lined with countless woodworking tools. 'Darn it Tommy, you're beginning to stretch my patience.'

'She was a very beautiful woman,' said the cooper finally, 'but I could only see her mouth. She wore a big cloak with a deep hood, dyed blood red and made of the finest silk. She kept her head bowed and eyes in shadow, but her words came from her lips like the softest of kisses. I can't put my finger on why, but I felt she was very sad, and I thought that even before she told me why she'd come.'

'And why did she want a barrel from you Tommy?'

'God damn, and what hell I may find myself in ...'

'Go on, Tommy.'

'She ... she wanted me to make a barrel that could hold happiness. That's what she asked for.'

'Holy Mother!'

'That's what I thought.'

'Right, that she'd lost her marbles. I hope you told her where to get off.'

'Well, I asked her what she meant.'

'And?'

'She wanted me to fill it up with laughter.'

'Now I know you've lost it.' The young man raised his voice. 'So, you just went ahead and said you would, did you? Christ alive Tommy. Then I s'ppose I'm your laughter machine, am I?'

'I guess I thought—'

'You're scraping the bottom of the barrel with me, ain't you?'

'Haha ... yes, haha!'

'That's it old man, have a laugh on me why don't you? Oh ... I get it, I didn't mean—'

The cooper rocked with laughter and slapped his thigh, a cloud of sawdust erupting from his apron.

The young man sniggered. 'It was 'cos she took a fancy to your barrel organ, wasn't it old man?'

'You've got me over a barrel with that one!'

The two men doubled-up and laughter echoed from every surface of the coopering shed, resonating deeply from inside the perfect oak barrel.

'Quick old man, the stopper, the stopper ... ha, ha!'

'What? Oh yes ... hee-ha-ha!'

'Here take this,' said the young man, slapping the handle of a wooden mallet into the cooper's trembling palm.

The cooper slammed in the stopper and hammered it home with a resounding "tonk".

The two men regarded each other a moment, their faces flushed red and eyes streaming.

'You see old man, once you told me, it were like shooting fish in a barrel weren't it?'

'You know son, you're a right barrel of laughs!' chuckled Tommy, clutching his sides and heaving a sigh of relief.

TREE ANGEL

I

༜

I was a fairy once, long ago. A fancy one too; there aren't many you
meet with opposable thumbs. I had every grace a good fairy
should have and more besides: glitter in my tightly coiffured
blonde locks, a sparkling tiara, and naturally enough, below my pink
mock-laced bodice, a dramatic candyfloss tutu. In my slender fingers I
flourished a stunning silver-handled wand topped by a five-point star
endowed with iridescent ribbon tassels.

It was a mundane existence, my lonely routine pierced by glimpses
of public adulation and festive cheer, but most of the year I was left
alone. To be frank, I was abandoned, in the dark, imprisoned and held
in solitary isolation in my box-like cell. They didn't mean to be cruel, I
knew that, just efficient in their war against entropy, in their keenness
to move on. Life doesn't stand still you know.

Beside the dark there was very little to stimulate my senses. An
occasional slammed door or muffled raised voice, a distant doorbell
or the dog barking at a visitor. My discomfort fluctuated during the
year. Most of the time I was frigid with cold, yet for just a few months
each year I would be baking hot, so hot in fact that I thought I might
melt into a puddle. When my fears overcame me, I imagined them
discovering me transformed; a pink tutu floating in a rectangular sea
of reconstituted plastic. But it was always at the coldest moment,
while the house was quietest, when life would dramatically improve,
and that little expectation kept me going through the worst moments.
Over the years I was able almost to predict the moment that the cold
and silence would be brilliantly banished.

The loft hatch would creak open without warning. First the dazzling
bright light would flood the dusty void, followed by a tsunami of warm

air, waves of perfume, baking, and wood smoke washing over me. That was the exact moment I longed for every year.

II

࿐

Back in those days, I took my fairy duties seriously. There'd be important guests coming round for Babysham and vol-au-vents stuffed with prawns. I'd keep calm during the final frantic hoovering, the argument over why he'd not checked the lights earlier, the capitulation when he found a spare bulb he'd bought last year for just such an eventuality. At the height of the party, I'd listen to him talking about work with his boss, even though I knew both of them would rather discuss anything other than the accounts and were trying to hear what their wives were talking about that was so hilarious. Up near the ceiling the cigarette smoke built up to near toxic levels and the plastic green leaves caused my back to itch in the heat.

There were rarely any children in the house, at least not until Boxing Day when the other family members came to visit. The little ones would open their presents in a dash and then be gone. She'd tell her sister that she shouldn't worry, that it was good for the two kids to play outside now that they were in the country for the day. The dog was always happy to have playmates, but they were wary of him and would rather he stayed inside with the grown-ups. One time, when the children had been called in to wash their hands before lunch, the older girl stood below staring up at me. She leaned forward to try and reach me with grubby fingers and almost toppled the tree, but I was saved at the last moment by a shouted command to come to the table.

Often a week afterward there'd be another party, this time with close friends. Talk of accounts or the commute, was replaced by gossip and intrigue, holidays in the planning, laughter and camaraderie. Eventually the party music would dim and the TV would be switched on so they could stand in a semi-circle and watch the hands of a big clock reach 12 o'clock, at which moment they'd share kisses, hugs and handshakes.

Occasionally though, at the very same time of the year, I was abandoned in silence, left staring down at an empty and dark living room. The fire which had been burning continuously for the last week burnt out, the tree lights turned off, and the dog banished to the kennels. Outside in the street I would hear explosions and cheers, but inside I may as well have been back in my box and up in the loft. Then I knew with certainty that I soon would be.

III

༄

Life changed irreversibly one year. I would like to say that I knew it would never be the same again as soon as the loft hatch opened, and an altogether different smell entered with the usual wash of warmth. I recognised the sweet scent of a young human and my mind raced at what that could mean for my routine. But really, I had no idea; no idea at all.

There were no work gatherings, no cigarette smoke, and only muted festive music. There was constant to-ing and fro-ing of family that I barely recognised. Neither I nor the tree were spared a second glance; even the dog looked put out. I lost my usual vantage because the tree was half its usual stature, although the crinkly and irritating plastic leaves were no more. I almost gasped when I was popped atop the prickly needles of a real tree, not that anyone appeared to notice the family's change in status.

Everyone's eyes were on the gurgling bundle of Louisa May, who later would let it be known that her name was Lou. Three years later, she was joined by Robert, who never became Rob or Bob. Every year after, I was amazed by how much the children had grown, and every year I would feel more that I was part of a real family. After eight Norway spruces—whose needles fell to the carpet like rain and clogged the old hoover—I realised that the family had finally graduated when I was nestled into the soft and scented needles of a six-foot balsam fir. That was the same year when my life really changed.

IV

୬୦

First of all, I gained a name. I didn't realise that Lou and mum were talking about me at first. It was only when the girl insisted that Gabrielle held a tree chocolate in her empty hand, and I felt my fingers being gently prised open and closed again around a crinkly foil wrapper.

The big day itself arrived and as always, I revelled in the excitement of the children as they followed the reindeer footprints from the front door to the fireplace and across to the gargantuan pile of presents below me and under the tree. Boxes were shaken, soft wrapping squeezed, and sneaky peeks made to the big presents hidden at the back of the pile behind the graceful drooping boughs of the balsam fir.

Stockings were opened first, warm milk downed and a boiled egg with smiling face smashed. Dad hurried in from the already cooking turkey looking frazzled, Mum was gathered from bed. The magic of the day took a firm grip on the family as they gathered below me, rubbish bag at the ready, blank paper and pen poised to make thank you lists, excited chatter from Robert and Lou.

After the socks, gloves, woolly hats, more socks, board game, books, monster eyeballs and smelly things, only the big presents from Mum and Dad remained. The youngest went first. A new engine and fleet of carriages for his train set. Then it was Lou's turn.

The girl could hardly lift the big box. Dad crawled forward to help. Lou tore off the flimsy paper—two whole sheets shredded in an instant—and I watched her stare in surprise at the words and pictures printed on the box.

Craft n'Style • Máquina de Coser • Machine À Coudre
Battery operated. Real Foot Pedal! Free patterns.
Sew like a Professional.

She was well brought up, and a split second later she made sure her face lit up to mask the disappointment as she rushed over to hug Mum and Dad.

V

꙰

The sewing machine was opened properly after lunch. Mum showed Lou how to use it while Dad read the instructions. Mum said Dad didn't know how to sew. Dad said that wasn't true, just not with a machine. Lou told them to stop arguing. Mum and Dad exchanged a look. The rest of the afternoon, and for the whole of Boxing Day while Dad snored on the sofa, the machine sat forlornly on the coffee table, a half-finished pony badge stuck under its needle. It reminded me of the hours I'd spent with a Norway spruce up my back.

I was woken up early next morning by the rhythmic rattle of the sewing machine. In between bursts of noise, I could hear Lou breathing hard through her nose, like she did when concentrating. She was busily crafting something with a small piece of blue denim. By her side lay a drawing she'd made of what appeared to be a doll wearing jeans. I was pleased for her. I had no idea what was coming.

Lou was to spend all day at the machine. Dad had to fetch fresh batteries and after a particular moment of angst, successfully changed a broken needle. The girl was so engrossed they had to shout three times for her to come for lunch. During the afternoon, she called for her mum and the two of them whispered together in a conspiratorial fashion. Lou told her to sshh while both stole a look at me. It was disconcerting. By the evening the doll's trousers were complete and Lou had started working with a piece of tartan fabric. I recognised the pattern from a pair of Dad's boxers that he'd worn while putting the cat out late one night. Mum told Lou not to worry, they had been washed.

The tartan creation took another day to complete. Halfway through the second morning, Lou had called her brother over and whispered a set of instructions to him. Her hands described something complicated, but I couldn't make out what it was. Robert left the room asking Dad if he had any brown paint. Lou shouted after him saying there was a lolly stick in the drawer he could use if Dad could help him cut it. Whatever it was that Robert was charged with making with Dad, they were working at it together in another room.

When it was time for bed, Lou wished me goodnight, singing my name as she ran upstairs.

VI

꤮

Early next morning, Lou plucked me from my fairy throne. She was so grown up she could reach the top of the tree just by standing on her tiptoes. As her big green eyes smiled up at me, I noticed that her hair was cut really short, and I wondered if she'd done it herself. I liked that she spoke to me all the time, reassuring me that this was a day I would never forget. She was right about that.

The first thing to go was the wand. 'You won't need this anymore!' The tiara and bodice followed in quick succession. 'There you go!' she exclaimed, my pink high heels tumbling to the floor as she whipped off the tiny tutu with a flourish.

As I lay prone on her warm lap, Lou was generous in explaining more about my transformation. 'You'll be much happier like this, won't you? And you'll never go back to that scary dark loft.' I was pleased with this news, but a little unclear what I was about to become happier about. I didn't have to wait long to find out.

I'd never worn trousers before, and my legs tingled all over as the scratchy blue fabric enclosed them. It was wonderful to breathe freely in the baggy tartan shirt, and Lou chatted to me as she rolled up its sleeves to just below my elbows. 'You won't be able to work with long sleeves, will you? There, that's better. Where did Robert put your work boots?'

She lifted me from her lap and held me out in front of her, and in a blur of snipping attended to my hair. 'You look so good, Gabe!'

Footsteps in the hall. A soft knock on the door. 'Hang on Mum, nearly ready.'

Lou jumped to her feet, thrust something into my wand hand and lifted me back onto the topmost branch.

'Come in, everybody!'

I watched from above as the rest of family traipsed into the living room, and at the very moment they all stopped and stared, I noticed what I held in my hand. 'What do you think?' Lou asked her parents. 'Your axe looks brilliant, doesn't it Robert?'

I looked down on their smiling faces, as Mum put a hand around Lou's shoulders.

'His name is Gabriel,' said Lou.

The three nodded in approval, looking to me, at Lou, and back again.

'By the way, you can still call me Lou,' said my young friend, 'but it's short for Louis. Okay?'

'Cool,' said Dad, sharing a glance with Mum. Robert was holding up his phone and taking pictures of me from every angle.

'He's going to live with me when he's not caring for the tree.'

'I'm sure he'll like that,' said Dad, nodding in approval. 'I've never seen a lumberjack fairy before.'

'Dad!'

'Honestly, can't you see he's not a fairy anymore?' interjected Mum quickly. 'He's a tree angel, isn't he sweetheart?'

'Yes, and although he won't be lonely anymore, his very favourite time of the year will always be Christmas.'

DARKNESS INTO LIGHT

I

&.

陰と陽

Soon after the Japanese forces flowed into the city and our inferior army withdrew in chaos, the lifeforces of two-dozen Japanese soldiers invaded a girl. Nine months later, on 4th September 1938, that 16-year-old brought me into this world. In this way my yang arose from her yin; do you understand?'

The branches of the ancient keyaki tree arching over our heads danced in the blustery wind. The delicate tip of one of its newly-emerged leaves stirred a pocket of dry soil lying between the exposed rocks. I strained to see the traditional characters the tree had painted in the dust, but a dust devil erased it before travelling in a swirl between our orange-robed knees.

'You are not ready to learn of these things.'

I narrowed my eyes against the gritty gust and shifted uncomfortably. I was still unused to sitting cross-legged for lengthy periods, and unfamiliar with his instruction; at once stern, yet steeped in kindness. He continued before I found any sense within myself.

'I did not ask you to take note of the tree's writing, nor the wisdom of the wind, but since nature has your attention, it is the yang in the force of air currents to which the tree bends and yields as yin.'

I nodded, trying to understand, running my fingers through my lengthening hair which lay damp against my perspiring neck. I studied his face. His silver eyebrows could easily have been modelled on the hairy caterpillars feasting above us, while his beard extended from his chin all the way to his folded legs as if sprung from the roots of the tree. When he scolded me, he never frowned nor raised his voice, but his green eyes sparkled with something which I had yet to fathom. It was never menace or anger, but while he looked at me it was like I had been summoned before twin fire doors opened to reveal the green flames of a copper smelting furnace. Then again, those eyebrows might be more accurately described as two natural bonsai pines clinging to a naked limestone face—

'I have had pre-pubescent boys half your age more able to concentrate!'

'I am sorry, Sensei,' I replied, feeling the intensity of his stare on the crown of my lowered head. 'I think what you describe is that for every action there is always an opposite action of equal force.'

I felt my pulse coursing down my legs and throbbing hideously in my numb feet. I had surprised him; perhaps he realised at last that I had real potential. At first, he had not wanted to teach me, but something I'd said or done during our first week together, now two months ago, must have convinced him to take me on, yet ever since I felt that I was a disappointment. I lifted my face fully expecting a benevolent welcome.

The furnace doors were fully open and, on his forehead—which warped as if gripped in the throes of an earthquake—the needles of the two bonsai trees were almost aflame. 'Do you think me ignorant of your Newton?'

'No, Sensei,' I stuttered, 'it's just that I've been taught about the laws of motion and it was easy for me to apply them to the things you've been saying.'

'Now you are concentrating,' he said, his face softening.

'Yes, Sensei.'

'1687, if I remember correctly.'

'That sounds about right,' I replied, trying to remember a lesson from my not too distant school days.

'Of course, you will believe that your Newton invented the concept, yes?'

'I think he defined them as laws of natural philosophy,' I answered proudly.

'Indeed. One day I will tell you about our natural philosopher Zou Yan. He defined the five elements, and the concept of yin and yang, two thousand years before Newton.'

I nodded, hoping that my 80-year-old teacher's attention had moved on from my obvious inadequacies. Beyond a curtain of whispering reeds, the little stream that fed the monotonous clacking of the bamboo shishi-odoshi, babbled and gurgled. The piercing cries of a golden eagle echoed in the gorge below and two oriental turtle doves were deep in conversation among the topmost branches of the keyaki. I watched a blush-pink breast feather make its slow way between the branches, weaving its way around one after another of them to settle on the ground between us.

'Do you see, Deshi?' he asked, his eyes on the feather.

'It's beautiful,' I answered.

'The feather is soft, yielding to gravity and the wind, falling passively, into the shade, resting now. The feather is yin. Everything about the feather is yin. The feather is like my mother.'

'So where is the yang?' I asked.

'The cock turtle dove focusses on the hen, active in his passion, sitting proudly in the sunlight at the top of the tree, free to fly into the sky to defy gravity whenever he chooses. Everything about the male dove is yang.' My sensei sat still for a moment, and I studied the tree limbs dancing in his raised eyes. 'Do you understand?' he asked eventually.

'I think so,' I replied. My mind tuned into the double echo of the shishi-odoshi. 'And your father?' I asked eventually.

The water tumbled out of the shishi-odoshi's bamboo spout and the old monk swivelled his head in time with the echo of its empty return, fixing his gaze on me. 'He was yang,' he answered simply.

'But he raped your mother.'

'Together with his friends, he raped Nanjing.'

'So ... ' I paused, 'the Japanese army was power, aggression, violence, probing ... taking not giving?'

'Now you show a little understanding, Deshi. The interaction of yin and yang is inevitable; every advance must be met by retreat, every rise by a fall, every push by a pull. Yin and yang transform each other. I was the yang that arose from the interaction between good and bad, and for my mother I was the happiness which came from grief, the fortune which grew from tragedy, an outer life which emerged from an inner death. In time, for a single moment only, I will exist at the pinnacle of yang, then I will fall and become yin.'

At a clatter of wings, I looked up to witness the female dove leading her mate up into the heavens. My glimpse of understanding fluttered away. I lowered my eyes to find my sensei looking intently at me, a benignant smile on his lips and a lively twinkle in his eyes.

II

陰と陽

It was George Harrison's doing, the whole idea of backpacking abroad, seeking enlightenment and myself before I might go to university. Unlike my favourite 60s band, I went alone, had no money to hire a guru and no preconceived idea of whom I should seek, only that I was drawn to the Far East. Maybe fate had drawn me along the four clattering hours from Hiroshima Station; maybe fate had brought my future sensei to queue next to me for a taxi. Perhaps there was the spark of yang in my stuttering Japanese that convinced him to offer me a casual job when I asked for directions to the temple.

I had tried to write home no less than four times. I wanted to tell my mother about the natural and unaffected beauty of the steeply forested mountains and my new-found happiness, but first I had to conquer my past. I knew I must put into words the pain of the past, explain my sudden departure and begin to apologise for all the anxiety that I had caused during my teenage years. I wanted to tell my mother that I now knew a little of these things, that I was beginning to know myself. In the dark of the night, memories of her defending me from social workers brought my heart racing to my mouth, and when I thought of her collecting me from the cells of the local nick after another public rampage, I squirmed with embarrassment, curling my knees tight to my chest. I needed to find the words to tell her how much I appreciated her over-stretched love. I needed to tell her that it was not her fault.

After a couple of months, even though I was still unable to write that letter, I had started writing. Sometimes single words or couplets came to me in the first vestiges of the day, before I began my duties at the temple. I learnt to record them, before they faded, in a small plain notebook. When I'd told Sensei about my new habit, he had nodded in approval.

I sat up in bed and shook the thoughts from my mind. Picking up the little notebook, I thumbed past several pages of scribbled words and phrases. As I turned to a fresh page to write that morning's gift, a leaf warbler burst into song outside my open window. 'Eagle | gorge, sunlight | chasm,' I recorded with the stub of my pencil.

I rose and dressed quickly in my simple robe and sandals. As I combed my hair back into a tight ponytail, which still felt strangely novel, I thought about how Mum wouldn't recognise me, rising at dawn, completing duties without complaint. I put a match to the small fire I'd prepared the previous evening and, while the small kettle warmed my shaving water, I brushed the wooden boards of my room, gradually moving towards the door and out onto the engawa. Although it was the height of summer, it was a cool morning as always. The temple and the collection of little wooden buildings clung to the ridge high above the north face of the Taishakukyo Gorge. Our situation was yang, my sensei had told me early on, before I had much comprehension. Mist rolled up from the falls far below, the echoes of its roars evaporating with the breath of the river as it met with the slanting rays of the sun just above our still and shadowed world.

I shaved quickly, knowing I must hurry to serve my sensei his breakfast of rice noodles, but something, some words, held me back. The image in my mind of an eagle soaring in sunlight above the dark chasm of the gorge compelled me to write more in my little book. Wiping my hands dry, I opened the notebook again and tried to write a haiku, but elegance and simplicity eluded me. I made three attempts, and while none satisfied me, I felt together that they achieved some kind of balance. Perhaps, I wondered, I'd invented a new form of collective haikai.

> *Roof of darkness torn,*
> *Razor wingtip searing dawn;*
> *Swirling yin and yang.*

> *Wing-tip tilted,*
> *Sunlight dipped in chasm shade;*
> *Yin wrapped yang.*

> *Dawn feathers golden,*
> *Soaring bright over darkness;*
> *Yang within my yin.*

I pocketed the notebook and hurried towards my master's quarters. As I scuttled round the corner of a building and made my final approach up a flight of steps, he raised a hand and urged me to stop, still many paces below where he sat meditating. 'Do you hear it?' he asked, his eyes raised upwards.

'It's a leaf warbler, Sensei, answering the one that sings outside my room.'

'And what is it they discuss?'

'Why I am always late?' I answered without hesitating. It had become our morning game, to wonder what nature thought of my learning.

He smiled and beckoned me over. 'Do you have something to read to me?'

I knew better than to ask how he knew, and with a nod I rested my fingers on the notebook tucked inside my robe. He motioned for me first to complete preparations for his breakfast.

As he tucked into his noodles, he asked me to sit and read. I waited for him to pause in his slurping before I began. After the first verse he sat motionless, and unsure of myself I paused before an almost imperceptible nod from him urged me on. I read the second and looked up again. The old man's eyes were softly closed as if his lids cradled the words before his eyes. Eventually, he nodded again, and I read the third verse aloud.

His remaining noodles went cold. The shadow of the gorge reached the apex of the temple roof. The leaf warbler retreated into shade. Finally, he spoke.

'They are not good haiku, Deshi. There is insufficient cutting.'

My heart sank.

'But your understanding of yin and yang shows promise.'

III

陰と陽

'I have a question, Sensei,' I said, pausing to gauge whether I should continue. We were sat together, as was our habit at midday, in the shade of the ancient keyaki tree. On one side lay the well-swept paving slaps and wide steps leading up to the temple, on our other a delicately-carved and sinuous wooden balustrade marked the divide between our sunny terrace and the deeply-shadowed gorge.

'Why did you come to Japan when its people brought such misery to your country and decimated your family?'

He regarded me for a moment, running his fingers down the fine white hairs of his beard. 'That is not the question you most want answered, is it Deshi?'

I should have known better, and my cheeks coloured partly from the bluntness of my question.

'The boundaries of yin and yang are constantly fluctuating,' he said, 'seeking balance and rebalance, but you have learnt that it is good within bad, yin within yang, which is the most powerful force for change.'

I gazed into the tree's spreading canopy seeking its wisdom in finding the answers I sought.

'You may ask again,' he instructed, after we'd sat in silence for a while.

'I can understand the nature of good and bad, heaven and earth, light and darkness, but things are rarely so simple,' I offered carefully, searching for an example. 'A whale must rise from the darkness to the surface of the ocean to breath, and sometimes will even break the boundary between water and air to fly completely through the air, if only for a fleeting moment. I think you will tell me that these are examples of constantly changing yin and yang, where always there will be balance, and that it's natural that this balance is ever-changing.' I paused to draw breath, frustrated by my inability to fully articulate the ideas swirling in my mind.

'These are good examples, Deshi, you understand that yin and yang flow in time as well as within an object. The whale creates a wave when it returns to the ocean which will be yang at its rising crest, and yin in its trough. Every object has both yin and yang, and they are not always opposite.'

'I think that I do,' I answered hesitantly.

'It is so within you, is it not?'

'I'm sorry, I don't understand.'

'You have changed more than you know. I have seen it with my own eyes.'

'How have I changed?' I asked, expecting him to talk about how I was calmer, more considered.

'You have come to terms with the brutality of your father, of the evil he did unto you and your family.'

I was speechless.

'You have had a mountain to climb, Deshi. In the case of my father, his evil was a legacy to me. For you, your father's evil was direct and personal.'

Tears welled in my eyes, and when the old man opposite me smiled kindly, there was nothing I could do to stem the flow of tears.

That night, I wrote a long letter to my mother. It was the hardest thing that I'd ever attempted and ultimately succeeded.

IV

陰と陽

'Deshi, when the keyaki is on fire, you should prepare to go home.'

I hadn't seen this coming. We were sat together in quiet meditation. I leaned forward and refilled his chá, placing the small earthenware teapot back on the bamboo tray. I felt his eyes watching my slow and considered movements, knowing that he approved.

'Sensei, you have changed my life.'

He smiled, but I could tell he had something more to say. I waited patiently.

Finally, he spoke:

> *The tree leaves signal,*
> *In flame red and limestone dust;*
> *A new beginning.*

'Do you understand, Deshi? The confluence of seasons, when light and dark sway one way or the other, where plenty meets poverty, and when love conquers hate, these are moments when life is at its very best, these are the moments to be cherished.'

I thought about this for a while and realised that the reverse was also true. It was quieter now that the river level had fallen in the gorge, and the babble of the stream near the buildings had dimmed to a tiny tintinnabulation. There was hardly a breath of wind, and the weary leaves of the keyaki hung in hushed silence. An orange-tip butterfly flew past, flashing its pure white wings and plucking the delicate strings of thoughts stretched between the two of us.

'Every time we sit here together,' I said, 'I think about the nature of this tree.'

He looked at me intently. 'That is why we meet here.'

'I have wondered about its balance. Half of the keyaki reaches for the light, defies gravity, and dominates our hearts and minds, and the other half survives only in the dark, obeys gravity, and is hidden from us. I don't understand how one life can be both yang and yin, but not change over time as you've taught me.'

'You see only the tree before you now, Deshi. One time, long in the past, a dove dropped a seed among these rocks, and it fell into a dark crevice. Without the damp and dark of yin, the vigorous yang of the shoot which emerged the next spring would never have come to be. Ever since, the roots of the tree have been in balance with its crown, even now while the tree is shrinking in old age.'

'It is the same with your appetite, Sensei.'

The old man chuckled. 'You are right, Deshi, otherwise my body would be too heavy for my feeble legs!'

V

陰と陽

'Last night, while I lay awake listening to the night life, a memory came back to me from my youth. Can I tell you the story, Sensei?'

It was our last meal together. The old man took another slurp of his noodles and nodded.

'The small village where I grew up was in the uplands of north Wales. Generations ago they mined the mountains for their slate which was sent far and wide, creating a roof for the engine of the country. The life of the miners was harsh, and we were told at school that children as young as five worked in terrible conditions, and these stories terrified me; I think I lived in fear that any day soon I would be sent down myself. Today, some of these old mines have reopened, but only for tourists, while the shafts and entrances of the others remain blocked. When I was a teenager, I decided to explore the open mines near the village. One day, high up the side of the mountain at the back of a previously unexplored cavern, and after clambering behind an enormous boulder at its throat, I found a tiny gap. It was very dark beyond, but I managed to squeeze through enough to discover that there was a cavernous space; I could hear the echoes of water dripping in the distance. The next day I returned with a torch, slipped through the gap, and turned on my light. The space beyond was so huge that my beam was swallowed by the soul of the mountain. Although I was scared, I proceeded into the darkness and my feeble torch only lit the way for my feet as I walked along the old mine track. Either side of my path the black disappeared into infinity. I felt like I was walking a tightrope. Eventually, I found a series of steep ramps, and I decided to scramble down one. At its bottom, I was surprised to find another old trackway from which more steep ramps fell away into darkness. I decided to descend again. At this point I had the sense to draw myself a little map on a scrap of paper that I had in my pocket, and I kept this updated as I explored deeper and deeper into the mine, eventually walking many hundreds of metres and descending five levels. Then my torch flickered and dimmed, and my predicament became suddenly clear; if the light failed, I would never find my way out and I would disappear from the face of the earth. I took a deep breath, turned off the torch to save its batteries, and sat down on a slanting slab of slate. At that moment, I felt the whole mountain weighing over my head, while the absolute blackness and total silence over-powered me.'

'I have never found such peace in my lifetime,' the old man said thoughtfully, taking a sip of chá.

'I thought that I might stay there for ever, Sensei. Now I realise that at that moment I was a tiny dot of yang at the heart of a mountainous yin. This place and your teaching have created the exact opposite, and now it is inside of me.'

The old man leaned forward and clasped my forearm. It was the first and last time that he touched me.

'I owe you a story in return,' he said, letting go of my arm.

'I'd like that, Sensei.'

'A lifetime ago, close to the border between two warring countries, a pretty girl was just entering womanhood when the fragile peace which protected her was cruelly shattered. The conquerors were ruthless, exterminating captured soldiers and killing civilians without remorse. The girl's ears were still ringing from the final artillery barrage when her home was burned to the ground by the invading infantry. Her father and brother were shot instantly, and her mother and grandmother bayonetted when they tried to protect the girl from being stripped. Her life was spared only long enough to satisfy the degenerate desires of the soldiers. She was not supposed to have survived, but by a miracle she escaped into the night, and eventually beyond the city walls. Two days later, miserable with grief and still in fearsome pain, she met a monk travelling in the same direction along the road that she fled. 'Don't worry,' said the monk, 'good things will come from bad.' And so it was, that eventually the young woman found herself in a village beyond the reach of the enemy, where she was welcomed and eventually gave birth to a healthy baby boy.'

It took me a while to realise the old man had stopped speaking. His eyes were fixed somewhere beyond me. The silence was broken by the gurgle of water and the dull clatter from the shishi-odoshi. I waited patiently for him to continue. *Splash ... tonk—tonk.* A cricket chirped. I closed my eyes. *Splash ... tonk—tonk.*

'Just after the war ended, a terrible illness swept through the region, and in the village the woman's son was the only child under five years old to survive the scourge. Many of the elders said that it was a miracle, but the boy's mother had tried to convince them to be cautious, saying "bad things come from good things." Indeed, just days later a young mother from a neighbouring village who had lost her only child and was now insane with grief, broke into the young boy's home intending to steal him, but she was spotted. During a frantic struggle, she stabbed his mother in the heart. As it was a poor village, no other family was able to take on the young orphan and a monk was called upon to decide what should be done. The monk spoke to the boy, who was very sad about the death of his mother, but when the monk said that he was sorry for the tragedy, the five-year-old wiped his eyes and said, "don't worry, good things will come from bad." The monk was surprised by the young boy's eloquence and asked him how he knew this, and the boy answered that it was something his mother always told him. And so it was, that the monk took the child into the family of the temple.'

I waited to be sure that he had finished his story. 'This was your early life, Sensei?'

'Like the ebb of the tide and the cycle of seasons, my life has since become a battle between yin and yang, of balance, change, and rebalance. I know that you will live a happy life, your glass always half-full. Follow the yin-yang way and make the world a better place.'

VI

陰と陽

Golden eagle wing,
Stirring light into darkness;
A life, positive.

FULCRUMOSITY

The table was the regulation two metres in length complete with a foot barrier halfway along its underside. A frown flickered across the girl's eyebrows. Even so, it was easy to read one of the few visible signs of emotion on her face beyond the mask which covered her mouth and nose.

'I read it on your profile of course, but just didn't know what it was that you actually do.' She paused, looking down at her hands clasped below the table. 'I can't say I'm any the wiser to be honest.' She raised her hazel eyes and stared back at him.

The two both held 16-week quarantine certificates and full genetic profile ID cards, otherwise they would not have been permitted to meet. It was a pleasant enough outdoor venue, fully cleansed and regularly patrolled by biosecurity, not that anyone would be stupid enough to try anything given the bristling surveillance tech.

'I read about this little wasp that only lives a single day,' he blurted. 'Basically, the male hatches, searches for a mate, does the deed, then dies.' He resisted the urge to touch his face; even with a lifetime of training it was hard not to give yourself a little comfort when stressed, even if you were fully aware of the dangers. 'If the whole history of this planet was seen through the 24-hour life of that wasp, you and I and all life that's ever been would appear in just the last second of the day. Crazy isn't it?'

'Are you always like this when you're nervous?'

The boy laughed, flushing pink, and the tension between them ebbed.

'So come on, tell me again, unless you study wasps?'

'That would make me an entomologist.'

She frowned again, but this time her eyes smiled too, and she cocked her head in mock annoyance.

'Sorry!' He held up a gloved hand as a peace offering. 'I thought you'd find it boring, that's all.'

'If we're to spend the next 16 weeks locked in quarantine together, then we might as well get the worst bits aired now, don't you think?'

'You think my job's my worse vice?'

'Seriously though,' she said, allowing a gloved hand to leave her lap to help express her feelings. 'Imagine being confined with someone that you found really boring, let alone a person you couldn't even have a decent conversation with.'

'It's amazing to have a face-to-face isn't it? I mean, I liked your profile and when we talked virtually that first time, I could tell we'd get on.' The boy paused a moment. 'You know, I really admire what you do, working with the infected.'

'I don't want to talk about it, if you don't mind?'

'Sure, sorry.'

'I'm trying to talk about you, remember? I'm beginning to think you're involved in crime, corporate espionage, or—'

'As if! I'm an environmental scientist. That's it really.'

A flock of ring-necked parakeets whirled overhead, clattering into a large London plane tree, its bright spring leaves just beginning to mask the city horizon. For the first time the pair of two young lovebirds looked away from each other, distracted first by the hideous squawking. At the same moment they both noticed the scene unfurling at the table next to them. They looked back at one another with mock fright, eyes wide and glancing pointedly at the nearby couple. A young woman leaned back in her chair with her arms crossed while her date sat sideways with his legs crossed and his eyes fixed on the parakeets.

'Maybe there's hope for us yet,' she said quietly. The girl and boy sat in silence a while, looking into each other's eyes.

'Humphrey Bogart is to blame you know?'

'What? Oh, I thought it was Jimi Hendrix.'

'This could be our first ever argument.'

'About the origin of London's parakeets?'

They burst out laughing. Noticing that the couple next door were now staring at them provoked further giggles, especially from her.

'They're a good example actually.'

'What?'

'Ring-necked parakeets are a good example of what I study. They've spread across the city since being taken from their habitat in Asia and unwittingly released into a new ecosystem. I've always been interested in natural history.'

'That's a weird term, don't you think?'

He waited for her to continue, eyebrows raised in expectation.

'You know, natural history, like it was something that used to be, a time long ago, no longer to be seen in modern life, something to be studied from the past.'

'I've never thought about it like that,' he replied thoughtfully, 'but you're right. It is weird isn't it? Particularly because the term was used before people were even aware of man-made climate change.'

'Yeah, almost like they subconsciously knew, even then, that the natural world would become history.'

'They were nearly right too, weren't they?'

'Yeah, but now we know nature has big teeth.'

'Why is it,' she asked, 'that all conversations eventually return to the same subject?'

'The one that no-one wants to talk about.'

'Umm ...'

'You're so easy to talk with.' He paused for a moment. 'I have to tell you, your eyes are beautiful.'

'Ah, thanks!' she said, turning to watch the unhappy couple leave in silence, breaking off in opposite directions to be met by two figures clad in white. 'Yours too ... nice I mean.'

They giggled, painfully aware of their awkwardness for a moment.

'Anyway,' the girl said finally, 'so far we've learned that you study dead parrots.'

'And you deal with dead ... sorry, I didn't ... I mean, I shouldn't—'

'It's okay. Don't worry about it.'

'No, it was stupid. What you said was really funny, and I ruined it.'

'Honestly, I'm used to it. Black humour helps us get through it all.'

Half the flock of parakeets rose from the tall plane tree and fell upon an ornamental cherry tree. Tears of white and pink fluttered onto the empty pavement.

'It helps to be curious, as a scientist I mean,' he said.

'So, other than parakeets, what are you most curious about?'

'Tipping points, that's my thing.'

'That sounds like an answer—finally!'

'If you really want to know, I'm a fulcrumologist.'

'I'm beginning to think I shouldn't have asked. What the hell does one of those do, other than tell strangers that their eyes are beautiful?'

'I study fulcrums in natural systems, although it's easier to explain by saying that I have a compulsive curiosity in fulcrums.'

'You mean that you suffer from fulcrumosity.'

'Ha!' he chuckled. 'That's genius. I've never heard anyone call it that. I am so going to use it.'

'Don't mention it ... No, I mean I do, like you know, you're welcome.'

'Are you really so nervous spending time with me?' asked the boy.

'Honestly, I'm not normally this bad. Reckon it's because I like you,' she blushed, apparently surprising herself by making the revelation out loud.

'Maybe I should tell you more about fulcrums before you decide, like unleash my full fulcrumosity on you?' It was the first time he'd said the word. He repeated it quietly under his breath, savouring its flavour and five wholesome syllables. He caught her staring quizzically at him, her dark eyes focussing on him as his lips explored the pattern of the word over and over again.

'Okay, try me.'

'If you're sure?' The boy barely paused. 'I was afflicted at university when I learnt about the Milankovitch Cycles, which explain the very long timescale variations in the Earth's climate, like our ice ages. It was a Serbian scientist who worked out that it was the planet's eccentric orbit round the sun, together with the Earth's tilt and wobble on its axis, which caused major periods of cooling.'

'Hang on, let me get that right; eccentricity, tilt, wobble. That's a cool fact.'

'Are you trying to be funny?'

'What, no I ... oh, that was genuinely an accidental pun.'

'If you don't mind, I'll get back to the science,' the boy teased. 'Anyway, it was Milankovitch that inspired me, 100 years after his discovery, to become an environmental scientist. I started reading everything I could about the predictable order in the Earth's natural systems that were previously thought to be only random or chance. The more I read, the more I began to wonder about chaos theory. It was German philosopher, Fichte, who in 1800 said something like "you can't remove a single grain of sand without changing the immeasurable whole." You've heard of the butterfly effect, right?'

The girl nodded.

'Well, if tiny changes can have untold impact, then big changes can push natural systems beyond thresholds from which they can't recover, setting loose uncontrollable and unpredictable chaos. Man-made climate change is a good example. These thresholds are called tipping points.'

'I like all this stuff, but I can't pretend that I know much about the theories. You could keep me entertained for a long time!'

'Right,' answered the boy, although he clearly wasn't really listening. 'Over time we had volcanos spewing out clouds of hot ash, occasionally disrupting the effects of Milankovitch Cycles, like when the Thames froze over every winter during the Little Ice Age. But then along came man and after a very short time, at least geologically speaking, we began to affect the planet's natural systems and finally our planetary climate. Anyway, to get to my point, it's the concept of the fulcrum, the point at which the levers of chaos and order pivot, that really began to excite me.'

'I can tell.'

'Sorry, but you did encourage me.'

'I was joking. Go on, it is interesting,' she winked.

'If you're sure. Think about you and me sitting opposite each other. The table could be the fulcrum, I could be order and you could be cha—'

'Hey, cheeky!'

'Anyway, we're in a delicate balance between what may be predestined or predicted by some forces of nature, versus some extraordinary or unimaginable event forced upon it by other factors.'

'You're telling me,' the girl joked, before more serious thoughts took over her mind. The boy looked equally pensive.

Finally, the girl spoke. 'I read an article recently that suggested it's our disruption of natural ecosystems which could be our greatest peril. The example was how we destroy forests, kill or capture animals that haven't had much contact with people, then sell them in wet markets.'

'Exactly!' the boy replied. So, it's no wonder that the viruses and other pathogens that existed on these animals are literally shaken loose from their natural hosts.'

'My dad used to shoot rabbits,' she said. 'I never forget him telling me how fleas on a rabbit almost instantly detect the tiniest reduction in body temperature of the dying rabbit and jump ship, taking a leap to the next nearest host, namely the hunter.'

'A small meal for man, a giant leap for flea-kind.'

'Ha, very good!'

'You're right though. It's just the just same with viruses when we destroy their natural ecosystems. We had Swine Flu, Avian Flu, Covid-19, Covis-21, and all the others before this one, and still we didn't seem to get how these zoonotic pathogens will fight to thrive, regardless of cost to human life. We keep building logging roads into the remote interiors of pristine rainforest, consume everything from our oceans, harvest meat from crowded factory farms.'

'So, you're saying that there's a sensitive fulcrum point in the planetary health system, not just where our climate can tip towards irreversible change, but a moment at which equally sensitive natural ecosystems may be disrupted to the extent that they pose a danger to the future of humanity?'

'I couldn't have put it better.'

'You're a bundle of laughs, aren't you?'

He smiled, despite the intellectual gloom. 'You know, I was really nervous about today, but honestly I already feel like I've known you most of my life. You're so easy to talk to ... and you have pretty eyes.'

'I think I prefer you when you're waffling about the global planetary health service.'

A figure in a white hazmat suit approached, disturbing the parakeets which shook more pink tears free as they took to the air squawking.

'Looks like our time's up,' said the girl, swivelling her head round to see what the boy's eyes were tracking over her shoulder.

She was a brunette he noticed; a few hairs had broken free from the elasticated hood of her suit, and were curled demurely over her forehead.

'Right then you two! Time's up,' spoke the all-in-white figure now looming over them. 'Have you decided whether to move forward to the next stage together?'

'I think we've reached the point of no return,' replied the girl.

PETRIFIED

W e walked along the cliff tops from town to town; about five miles wasn't it? We'd not known each other long; perhaps a couple of weeks, if not a little less. It had been raining and my trainers were soon covered in mud; no idea why I remember that. After the gentle stroll arm-in-arm along the seafront, passing between the screaming gulls fighting for Saturday night takeaway leftovers near the locked-up pier, we climbed the hairpin bends of Constitution Hill. It was busy with locals and students as there was nothing else to do on a Sunday. As soon as we left the gravel surface behind and headed north, we had the undulating cliff path to ourselves.

In Wales, everywhere used to shut on the Sabbath didn't it? Our destination was like a ghost town, but we managed to find a newsagent open only for the morning to sell the Sunday papers. We bought a couple of cold pasties, a large chocolate bar to share, and a couple of cans of fizz. Then we headed out towards the beach.

I didn't tell you that I had a reason for choosing that stretch of coastline for our walk. Winter had signalled its intentions with a fearsome storm the week before; sea spray even reached the first-floor window of your student digs, didn't they? We'd cuddled together drinking tea and watching the huge waves crashing over the pebble beach. We both wore our thickest woolly jumpers because that enormous bay window was draughty as hell. That's when the idea came to me because I realised what this display of raw power might just be revealing further along the bay.

We soon enjoyed the vista of beautiful wind-swept sand stretching out before us. There were four lonely miles ahead and no one to share it with except each other. Half a mile in the distance, the huge expanse of grey sand was interrupted by a dark shadow which spread its roots into the gentle waves and the ebbing tide. My heart skipped a beat; I might just have gambled successfully. I thought you'd understand my enthusiasm when we got there; what else would you expect from a budding biogeographer.

We walked hand-in-hand, and I remember that I couldn't stop

looking at you. Your red hair flowed over your shoulders as if you were Boudica riding a chariot along the sands. You would mock frown, knowing I was studying you, before I'd check myself and say something to cover my tracks. Your smiling eyes sparkled like the wavetops in Cardigan Bay.

As we grew near my heart beat faster, and not just because of you. I was right, it had been revealed by the storm! The blurry shadow had become a speckled cluster of dark shapes rising from the pale sand. Waves broke gently against those that were half-submerged.

You recognised it for what it was; after all it wasn't just your looks that mesmerised me. The blackened stumps of the petrified forest extended all round us. We stopped next to a large stump which reached up to our knees and I inhaled your scent as you leant close to watch me clear the bright green seaweed and point out its ancient rings. You listened politely while I told you about the oak trees which thrived 5,000 years ago, the evidence for giant auroch, of raised walkways built from hazel coppice by Bronze Age people, and even the fossilised footprints of their children weaving between the stumps.

Then it was your turn to surprise me. You told me about the legend of the fertile low-lying kingdom of Cantre'r Gwaelod and sang me the full version of *The Bells of Aberdyfi*. I recognised the lilting tune from many nights spent enjoying folk music in Welsh pubs but had never previously grasped its meaning. You taught me about the supposed drowning of 16 villages when the fair maiden Mererid was distracted by the amorous advances of a visiting king and had failed to shut the great gates which were meant to keep the sea at bay. Your silky voice spun a web between the stumps of the ancient forest before entrapping me.

We walked on, reaching the end of sands where they met the mouth of Dyfi. Two rusting cars lay half-submerged in the estuary mud; the hazard warning signs of rapid tidal currents apparently unheeded. I told you a story then, set long into the future when petrified metal remains mystified future palaeomechanics and inspired a great legend of the ancient time when cars ruled the world.

As we made our way back, the dark storm clouds we'd watched approaching across the huge bay finally reached us and within minutes we were totally drenched. We passed by the petrified forest, now being reclaimed by the rising tide, pausing briefly to listen out for the tolling bells but they were taken by the wind. We hurried on towards the town. We decided to head to the little station and catch a train back to our hometown but were dismayed to learn the next one was a two-hour wait. It was a Sunday after all.

In the station waiting room, which we had to ourselves, I sat on a bench next to the only radiator and you perched on my knee. Our wet clothes began to steam but when you started to shiver, I urged you to join me in a game of footcan with one of our empty tins. We played until the train arrived by which time we were almost warm although totally exhausted.

Within minutes of pulling out from the station you'd fallen asleep with your head on my shoulder, your gorgeous hair tickling my face. I watched Mererid's tears trickling diagonally across the carriage window as the Welsh countryside rushed by. It was only a 15-minute journey but by the time we'd arrived back in our university town, I knew, I really did. I'd never met a girl like you; a woman like you. I'd never felt about anyone like this in my twenty years. This was real love, not puppy love or infatuation love. This was love that would last a lifetime. I was flooded by rolling emotions and I was petrified.

WILD CHILD

S he knew where she was, even without opening her eyes. The roar and rumble of the motorway traffic rushing below was strangely comforting. Marianne came to this place with her mates most days after school, but not so much in the holidays. The bridge must've been built for some reason, but fuck knows what. You had to fight your way through thorns and shit to find it, even before squeezing through the hole cut in the locked wire gates. You could still see the tarmac, even the white lines down the middle, but it was cracked all over and plants had sprouted everywhere. It was much greener than when she first started coming five years ago. Now there were little bushes growing out of cracks everywhere; as there were on her own body. There were butterfly bushes in the brick parapet and a birch tree—like the one which filled her tiny garden—thrust upwards between two Catseyes. Even though she'd grown a lot herself, the once tiny tree was now way taller than her. She'd not mentioned her connection with the tree to her friends, but she'd told Stu to stop hitting it with a stick last time they'd all come together.

It was a bright summer's evening and she opened her eyes warily when something buzzed loudly over her head. Her eyes focussed instead on the empty condom caught in the tall weeds. It moved like one of those windsocks at the air base. Josh lay next to her, his head on her jumper, still out of it.

She had been wet even before she'd told Josh she was on the pill and he'd yanked the condom off. It'd been much better than the first time, in the back of his Dad's car just over a week ago. If he'd lasted a bit longer she'd've enjoyed it even more. He'd said going bareback made him too excited. She'd felt the same but hadn't said nothing. Josh'd pulled down her jeans and g-string just enough so they could do it, on all fours in the middle of the bridge, like animals.

After, they'd lit up, that's when she'd had the idea. He was slow to react and got the wrong idea when she'd lowered her jeans again. 'No, help me up stupid!' she'd said, slapping his hand away from her damp thighs. 'Now lean on my legs will ya, and don't' let fucking go.'

She'd shuffled backwards over the parapet and almost immediately felt the rush of wind from a truck as it sped underneath. The updraft was a blast. The next one to pass below honked its horns, and others did the same. 'They're getting a right fucking eyeful!' Josh had shouted. Then she'd felt another new sensation and peered down between her legs just in time.

'Holy shit!' she'd screamed, nearly falling backwards. Josh had tugged her hard and they'd fallen together onto the cracked pavement. She'd laughed 'til it hurt, and then had farted which only made it worse. His reaction didn't help either; 'what, what?' he'd asked stupidly, over and over.

Eventually, she'd got her breath back. 'I only just dropped our love gunk onto some fucking executive's speeding BMW!'

'Imagine his face!' laughed Josh. 'Like he had a boner when he saw your little arse but then his fucking windscreen got splatted on by some shitting giant bird!'

Only another pinner had dulled the pain in her sides, and they'd laid together giggling before they'd drifted asleep side by side.

Marianne watched the furry bumblebee land on a pointy cluster of deep purple flowers hanging from a bush growing out of the pavement. Clouds of white and orange butterflies fluttered round the bush which hummed with little bees. Something caught her eye, over her shoulder. *What the fuck's a dog doing out here?* Then she noticed a bushy tail. The fox looked right at her, its ears swivelling nervously, but it seemed less interested in her than something else. It looked ahead to the other side of the bridge, and Marianne slowly moved her head to follow the fox's stare as it started forward. *Oh my god, there's a fucking deer!* It was a proud fucker with huge antlers. Its ears were moving too but flicking away small clouds of flies that followed its strutting head as it started to cross the bridge towards Marianne and the fox. The two wild creatures were on parallel but separate paths and continued towards each other. They arrived together near the middle of the bridge. The deer shook his head and its antlers waved in a blur. The fox lowered itself, its belly scraping the tarmac, ears pinned back, before darting on and melting into the bushes on the far side. The stag continued towards Marianne; she held her breath until he was so close, she might almost have touched him. Then Josh stirred. In a heartbeat the stag crashed past them. Marianne saw the terror in the white of its eye.

As they walked hand-in-hand back into town, Josh eventually had to tell her to shut up about the fucking fox and the dumb deer. Soon after they'd split, each heading their separate ways, she'd felt more of his cum trickle out. It made her laugh out-loud and she got stared at by a lecherous jerk cocooned in a black Beetle among the crawling traffic.

'You're fucking late!' greeted her as she let herself in, closing the front door on the birch tree in the front garden and the outside world. 'Fish and chips.'

'Ta Mum,' Marianne shouted, carefully lifting the loaded plate from the hot oven. She hoped a generous dollop of ketchup would help revive the black-edged potatoes and shrivelled fillet.

Marianne slumped into her favourite armchair, tucked her legs under herself and balanced the scalding plate on the side of her knees. With her fork she stirred the crispy mushy peas. 'Never guess what I saw today.'

'What's that, inside of a book or som'it?'

'Funny! I saw a fox and a deer meet above the motorway.'

'You been smoking that shit again, Marianne?'

WOODCOCK MOON

Mother nature was beautiful; at her stunning best if I might be so bold. The evening light fell softly over her rounded contours, casting a golden warmth even among the shadowed dells near the feet of her arboreal children. A line of naked beech trees stretched languorously along the otherwise lonely ridge, a gentle breeze lifting their limbs to sway in unison with time immemorial. A bumble bee, muzzy with cold, crawled back under the crispy leaf litter beside me while overhead a homeward-bound red kite bid another day farewell.

I had this indefectible place to myself—other than the birds and bees of course—and at the perfect time to catch my favourite bird; crepuscular in habit, highly secretive, and perfectly camouflaged among the forest furnishings. *Scolipax rusticola* might as well be an alien lifeform given how few people would recognise one even if they were fortunate enough to stumble upon one. They'd get a twilight fright they too, as a woodcock will sit tight until the unwary's foot is almost within a step of falling upon its back before suddenly fleeing in a startling zig-zag and a blur of wings.

I'd waited until the Woodcock Moon—the first full moon of November—when high numbers of new birds were expected from across the North Sea, freshly arrived after their long and dangerous migration from Russia. A charming legend says they are guided on their way by our tiniest bird, the goldcrest, who will ride as a navigator on a woodcock's rounded back, nestling between its wings.

It was surprisingly warm for the late autumn evening, but I was wrapped up well in readiness for a long wait and had already enjoyed a warming cup of cocoa from my thermos. I'd chosen a vantage point near the ridge overlooking the woodland edge and a large clearing. I sat motionless against the trunk of an ancient beech, its tightly wrinkled and mossy bark blending perfectly with my birding jacket, and I watched the sun begin to set over the low fields to the west, half-hidden under a blanket of mist.

A young lady came strolling into the clearing and immediately looked out of place. She looked eastern European I thought; please don't think that I'm a racist, I mean that she was dressed strangely for a ramble in the countryside. One moment she had been on a fashion catwalk and the next had been … what did they call it on that Star Walk programme … teleported, that's it. She carried a small backpack and wore a pair of stout leather walking boots while her long legs were entirely bare, her modesty protected only by the shortest of denim shorts. Her top half was more appropriately covered by a black quilted jacket, its fur-rimmed hood pulled up over her head. I studied her through the 8x40s, and when she swept aside a lock of tumbling golden hair, I noticed she was talking to herself, or more precisely talking to someone even though she was completely alone. It reminded me of the way the young have of talking to their phones while walking down the street with those wireless earpieces. It's taken me a while to get used to the habit; at first, I thought there were an unusually high number of people in our little town with some form of schizophrenia. This young lady was acting up, smiling and making other gestures to suggest that her imaginary friend could see her. Then I realised that what I'd thought was a walking stick had something attached to its end. It was evidently a small camera and she was filming herself.

I watched her make her way towards a fallen beech trunk at the centre of the clearing. She almost danced her way there, pirouetting and lifting her shapely legs, and all the while smiling to her camera. The stick metamorphosised into a tripod which she set up carefully atop the giant log. She must have paused the camera then because she stopped smiling and began to look nervously about, clearly making sure that she was without company.

At this moment I admit that I was entirely unsure what I was to do. I was some distance away and well-enough hidden that she wouldn't spot me if I kept still. For a moment I thought that I might try to slip away quietly because I felt I was intruding on a private moment. What stopped me? I think partly, I didn't want to startle her, but I have to admit that I also didn't want to lose my perfect woodcock perch. I didn't expect her to linger long as she'd soon catch a chill, so I made the decision to stay. If only I'd known the events which were to unfurl, I might have reconsidered my voyeuristic position.

My muse, in the sense that she inspired me to write this story—so let's call her Erato—was smiling again as she backed away from her camera. She stopped a few feet away from it, centred perfectly in a glowing crystal of dusky orange. With barely a pause she removed her jacket and let it fall to the shadows on the forest floor. My eyes followed it briefly before being drawn back to her startlingly pale form, lit by the glowing evening sun. She had been completely naked under her jacket, and now began to run her hands seductively over her bare chest, her golden hair tumbling over her narrow shoulders. With barely a wiggle, the denim shorts followed, until there was her full moon, apparently as nature intended.

During the next 20 minutes, I bore witness to things that I'd never imagined, let alone seen during my 55 years of happily married life. I learnt during an instance of particularly acrobatic urination, that her rear orifice was plugged by a bejewelled phallus. In another dazzling display, Erato was able to make a water bottle completely disappear from view, and on completion of an elegant cartwheel along the trunk, she was able to reveal it again in a magician's flourish to camera. Her performance of the love arts came to a close only after she'd straddled the smooth hardwood log and rocked her hips rapidly to and fro with a view to achieving an evidently satisfying conclusion to the evening's activities.

I can honestly say that during the entire display, all thoughts of woodcock had slipped my mind, and it was only when the show was over that I noticed that the sun had finally dipped below the horizon. She worked quickly now, her smile replaced with business-like efficiency. Baggy tracksuit leggings replaced the shorts, and she pulled a dark woollen beanie hat hard down over her ears. With camera and tripod last to be packed away, Erato made to leave after a last look around.

I glanced away, perhaps to check the time, but almost immediately was startled by a piercing scream. My heart skipped a beat. I raised my binoculars just in time to see a blur of wings from not one, but a trio of woodcock flushed by my startled muse.

A mere five thousand miles to fly;
Rising from the Russian steppe,
And guided by a crest of gold,
To fall upon the English cold,
On the night of the Woodcock Moon.

TALL STORIES
SHORT TREES

I 've always thought that reading a story on an e-reader is like being too close to a tree; you can't stand back and admire the whole wood. It's difficult to sense where it begins or where it ends. You can't feel its true volume or enjoy that smell after you've accidentally left it outside overnight. I suppose it's the difference between seeing a forest on a TV documentary, and standing in one yourself as the drizzle dampens your hair and the midges worry your brow. Don't get me wrong, I love the convenience of an ebook and mostly read on one myself, but sometimes it's good to see the wood for the trees, if you get my nature?'

Now he thinks I'm some sort of literary chatterbox. Me and my big mouth.

We head out across the tussocky moor, walking side-by-side, soon slipping into silence as the slope steepened, our noses following the scent of sea mist.

'I read a book of short stories once in which every one of them was about trees,' I say as we gaze back down the featureless slope, interspersed here and there by a sheep with its head down among the deciduous brown grass. 'The author must have had a real obsession about them. Called "Tall Stories Short Trees", or something like that. Maybe you know it?'

Oh, what've I said now?

'"Tall Trees Short Stories", yes, that was it.'

'Oh really, you're the author? Wow!'

At least you didn't put your foot in it.

'You've written quite a few books then?'

'Impressive. They say there's a book in everyone, but I've not found mine yet. Reckon it's like trying to catch the wind with a net in my case.'

'I assume your next one's about trees, otherwise why else would you have asked me to accompany you on this mission?'

Doesn't say much, talk about getting blood from a stone. Perhaps all authors are the same; like there's a finite number of words and he's saving them for the page rather than wasting them on me. Probably nothing personal.

'Careful now, there's a stretch of bog in front of us here.'

'So, where did you learn to abseil?'

'Mountain rescue. Where did you serve?'

Must be an expert at bogs then! Won't bother pointing them out anymore.

'A place of misty moors like this but without the jagged peaks. Beautiful place, not that I know it well. Guess you dealt with people getting lost and hypothermic rather than climbing injuries and the like?'

'I've been a climber all my life, so I'm more into rocks than trees.'

'Coming across a tree out here is like discovering a hen with teeth.'

'What species did you say we're hunting today, a something bus?'

'A rare form of whitebeam. Right.'

'One of only six known in the country, really?'

'Like finding a willow tree growing grapes, or a shoal of fish climbing a poplar tree!'

'I've no idea, just my weird mind. Sorry.'

He'd been gone five minutes. The rope was still taut and I could feel him moving to and fro below.

Famous tree author falls to death discovering rare tree ... God I've a twisted mind!

I cast my eye over the climbing equipment again before looking out across the spectacular view. Most of the sea was fractured by scudding shadows but a single shaft of sunlight cut through the gloom to highlight the mare's tails of the choppy water in the middle distance. A storm was brewing. The frantic song of a Dartford warbler erupted from the nearby prickle of gorse, accompanying the echoes of the booming waves striking the base of the cliff 200m below.

✄

'You'll be able to write a tall story about that short tree won't you?'

He'd climbed back up looking knackered, face flushed from a combination of effort and exposure. The warbler had fallen silent, but the booming waves were unrelenting. He didn't seem to appreciate my humour.

'Looks like the rain's coming in. Shall we head away from the edge? That thicket halfway down might lend us a little shelter.'

I coiled the ropes and packed away the equipment while he scribbled some notes in a small book. I noticed some attractive lobed leaves, their greens fading to yellow at the margins, tucked carefully between pages of tiny handwriting and thumbnail sketches.

The deluge came well before we reached the shelter of the trees, but we pressed on with heads down. The rough terrain made the going painfully slow. The skylarks were larking no more and had gone to ground.

I blew on my cold wet fingers before fumbling to open my rucksack. We were shielded from the worst of the driving rain by the contorted shrubs.

'Chocolate?' I offered, before pouring a cup of steaming black coffee into my mug.

Bet he'd rather be making notes than talking with me. No choice in this weather, Bud.

'Would you call this a thicket or is there a more technical term, like a copse or something?'

'Spinney. That's a new one for me.'

'These are hazel trees, aren't they?'

'We're in a madhouse of hazelnuts.'

Damn, he actually smiled.

I looked across to my companion. His woolly hat looked sodden and a permanent drop of moisture hung from the tip of his nose. He looked happy, like he was in his element.

Like a flotilla of oaks, a perfumery of guelder roses, a pack of dogwoods, a tangle of spindles, a journey of wayfarers ... I could have fun with words like these.

'So how did you start writing?'

He looked out across the windswept moor without answering, before turning to look at me. 'I unfurled my net,' he answered with a smile.

FRAGMENTS

Trunk, limb, bough, branch, twig, leaf, blough. Don't you see Margaret, it's as though the words themselves were perfectly crafted by the geniuses of Fibonacci or Leonardo da Vinci? Curling from ground to tip, tapering from substantial to ethereal, visible to invisible.'

'Well, I suppose, but surely you can't just make up a word, Ann.'

I studied the familiar shoreline of my old friend's frown, watching ripples of uncertainty drift across her brow, the fear of wading in too deep written clearly across her face.

'Why not?'

'Because there are rules, and dictionaries, and convention, and—'

'I'm not doing any harm, and no one has to use the word if they don't want to. If I was a fashion designer, I wouldn't expect everyone to like my creations.'

'That's different. Honestly Ann, since you've started writing you've become ever so ... so bold.'

We sat side by side in silence for a while, looking out across the expansive park, its barren green playing fields stippled here and there with russet and yellow shadows of naked trees. Our attention was captured by the screams of a small boy being spun faster and faster on a roundabout until his dad stumbled and fell. A bank of discarded leaves that had been resting against the equipment and then stirred into a swirling cloud by their play, began to rain down on them both. The man brushed the knees of his trousers with his hands, chuckling as he picked brown leaves from his hair. The boy's hilarity was infectious. I sensed my friend relax and watched the imprint of a smile appear on her temple, as though a jay had skipped lightly across the side of her face.

Beyond the father and son duo, a leaf devil appeared, heading towards our bench, whipping golden plane leaves several feet into the air as it passed between the swings. At my feet the blough trembled in anticipation as if electrically charged. The draught lifted my skirt, while pine needles, peduncles and petioles tumbled across the toes of my leather walking shoes. A small black beetle appeared between our feet, landing on its back among fragments of shattered samara. For a terrifying moment its six legs frantically sought traction before the creature received a glancing blow from a tumbling horse chestnut husk. It scurried under the arch of Margaret's sensible town shoes.

'There's life within blough!'

'Pardon?' asked Margaret, swivelling her body stiffly to gaze at me.

I hadn't realised the thought had escaped me. I hoped the beetle might have survived my fellow titan's seismic shift. There was no sign of it among the stalks and twiglets.

'You've told me virtually nothing about your writing,' she sighed. 'I have to admit I'm actually quite intrigued,' she added in a barely audible whisper.

The distorted hour chime from the church steeple reached us across the rolling green. A trio of jackdaws took to the air noisily from the skeleton of the nearest tree. Their shadows darted towards us before fading suddenly as the sun was snuffed out by a speeding cloud. A wren began to tick angrily from the dense hazel stems behind our bench.

'Three o'clock. School will be out soon,' said Margaret, tightening the knot of her head scarf. 'I can't believe that nowadays they allow them to ...'

Of course, blough contained not only the spent and the dead, but the living. Spiders and their silken cocoons, fungal spores, beetle eggs, homeless feather mites, seeds seeking scarification. Life passing by, life in waiting, life in motion.

'Don't you agree—Ann, have you been listening to a word I've been saying?'

'Yes, yes of course I have.'

Squirrel lashes, woodpecker talon sheaths, wood mice waste, iridescent feather barbs, thousand-year-old heartwood dust, day-old drosophila dead already.

'You're so very pensive, Ann.'

'I was just thinking more about blough.'

'I can tell. You've not heard a word I've said, and it's no good you saying otherwise.'

'Sorry. That's the most surprising thing about writing. Thinking is just as important as typing. Sometimes, I just know a thought is worth pursuing and that I mustn't let it escape. Anyway, you asked about my story, I'm sorry, Margaret.'

'If you don't mind talking about it?'

'Sometimes, don't you feel just so small and inconsequential?'

'Well, I suppose—'

'Fighting to stay upright, to stay alive against the odds?'

'Tch! Honestly Ann, I can't say I think like that very often,' she said, drawing her jacket tightly about herself.

'It's an effort staying alive, simply unnatural, because the default is death. A jump or a flight can never last forever. Everything returns to earth, everything dies; death is the *status quo*. Only from the earth and from death comes life.'

'You are so terribly morbid sometimes, Ann. I hope your story is more uplifting.'

'I suppose blough is like primordial seasoning, but that's not how I saw it in the beginning.'

Parents began to stream through the park with blue and grey uniformed children. A young woman passed by, deep in conversation with an animated girl in a plaid skirt, a colourful drawing waving violently in the child's free hand. A father pushed a buggy complete with laughing toddler up and down the grassy mounds in pursuit of his schoolboy brother. The wildlife had melted into the long shadows, finding solace in the crannies, or safety in the treetops.

'How do you spell it?'

'Sorry?

'Bluff, as in a small cliff or—'

'No, blough, as in soil that can slough off a bluff.'

'Oh, with a "gh"?'

'I thought so.'

'But can you invent a word, just like that? Won't your editor strike it out, even if you won the battle with your word processor or whatever it's called these days?'

'I don't see why not. It's no different than a company coming up with a brand name that becomes so ubiquitous it enters everyday language. The real innovation is happening at the sharp end of our culture.'

'That's not for me, that social whatever,' said Margaret.

'I rather like it. I've got 250 followers now.'

Margaret swivelled her head around deliberately. 'Well, I don't see them.'

We both chuckled.

'And why a word for the ... well ... tree chaff and other microscopic bits and bobs, the gubbins and appurtenances of nature which are everywhere around us?'

'I think you've answered your own question! That's a great word by the way, appurtenances. I might use that.'

Margaret smiled smugly. 'I suppose there is a lot of blough. Perhaps it does deserve its own word.'

'Exactly. After all, it is a word describing the origins of life,' I replied, pleased that I'd won her round. 'They got it wrong in the old scriptures; it's not dust to dust. Amazing really that we've never had a word for the most important substance of life; a term for an existential phenomenon.'

'Don't tell me that you're writing an entire story about blough.'

'Just fragments. A gentle and ordinary story about life, where everything is inconsequential and temporal. A miscellany of natural paraphernalia of minor consequence, other than being about the origins of life of course.'

'But who would enjoy reading a story like that, Ann?'

'I suppose I'll find out in time.'

And eventually the hardware will become obsolete, the software unintelligible, the printed pages soluble or flammable, our data centres and great libraries reduced to rubble and dust, the intellect, theories and ideas churned to dust, blowing in great dunes for millennia, baked into sedimentary foundations for future civilisations yet somewhere surely, a fragment of life will prosper and flourish again from the blough.

THE WIPERS TREE

I

⁂

H arry was extraordinary. Among the many thousands, if not tens of thousands of other Harrys—not to mention the countless Arthurs, Harolds, and Alberts—everyone knew which Harry you were talking about when you said, 'Reckon I just saw Harry hurry past'. Some people called him 'Old Harry' because he was a veteran alright, but mostly it was just Harry, or more likely 'arry. He even featured in The Wipers Times. You see, Harry was different to all the other men because he was a pigeon.

I should also say that Harry was no ordinary pigeon. It was only years later that people discovered that he was actually a she, but that's not the main point to this story. What made Harry special was that he served as a homing pigeon on the Western Front for two years, whereas most of the serving birds survived only months or weeks, if they were lucky. Most of the 20,000 poor feathered beggars serving on the front copped it, and copped it bad.

I served as a corporal in one of Osman's pigeoneer squads, and the story I have to tell is about the battle where I nearly lost my life and was lucky enough to come home with a single working leg and my sight in one eye. It was 1917 and the Third Battle of Ypres, but you've most probably heard of it as Passchendaele I imagine. It was the battle where the Allies finally got some of their ducks in a row. We had effective tanks while the Huns had virtually none. I went forward in a tank once and had to release a bird every 100 yards through a little porthole in the side gun turret; scariest thing I ever experienced, being in that pressure cooker. We also had flamethrowers, Vickers machine-guns, Stokes mortars, and rifle grenades a plenty, while our heavy boys had perfected the creeping barrage.

Anyway, I was about to tell you about the attack on Polygon Wood. I don't know if you've ever seen any pictures from the time, but though it was called a wood, you must know it was no more than fractured tree stumps and upended root plates surrounded by deep craters half-filled with water, the rest of them taken up with tangled barbed wire and the bones of the dead. We made our way up the Menin Road towards Ypres early in September and our little unit spent time sending non-urgent messages from behind the frontlines back to headquarters. We knew then we were being fattened up for something big.

Private Watkins—that was my buddy because us pigeoneers always worked in pairs—wasn't into birds like I was. Don't misunderstand, he was good with them, but he wasn't a fancier like me. He would pull my leg about it all the time, even while the Hun were taking their best aim at us. You might think he would be more respectful of my rank, but it wasn't like that in the pigeoneers, unless an officer was round and about, naturally. Stuff like 'bird brain, or 'feather head,' and the like. He was a damn good cook though and made the fastest brew of any I served with, plus he had a knack for having a tot of something strong to slip into it more often than not. No idea where he got it half the time.

People don't realise today how important them birds were. They could relay a complex message quicker than any telegraph back from the frontline. It might take as little as six minutes for a message carried by a pigeon from the frontline to fall right into the hands of a general or his staff back at headquarters. There was no technology that could beat them. The thing was, they needed to be right at the heart of the action while all the time be handled with love and care, and that's where us pigeoneers came in.

Watkins and I finally learnt our fate the night before the big push when we were ordered to join a unit of Anzacs on the right flank. We were to be in the first wave leaving at the first hint of daylight. It was to be a great surprise to the Hun who were going to be softened up by a huge barrage by the heavies only minutes before. We'd be following up closely on foot behind the terrible wave of destruction left by the 18 inchers. They were brave soldiers those Australians, and they knew how to wile away an evening, even though every man's gut must have been wrenching inside like mine was. I wrote a long letter home to Mother and Father that night, sitting in the relative comfort of the cab of the converted old London bus that served as our mobile pigeon loft. My last job before turning in was to select the twenty birds for each of the two-tiered wicker baskets that Watkins and I would wear strapped to our backs to carry the birds forward.

II

I remember shaking hands with Watkins. We looked each other in the eye, holding each other's gaze for an uncommonly long moment. We both knew what was at stake. 'Good luck, old chum,' I said. I remember distinctly his reply to this day. 'In this life or the next, at least we'll have the birds to carry us to heaven.' It was most unusual for him to be serious like that, let alone be so poignant.

Just minutes later, Watkins exploded in a puff of grey feathers. One moment he was on my left side about 30 yards away, and the next, I was blown off my feet by the shell, and as the mud came down in a filthy rain onto my tin helmet, I looked in vain at where he had been advancing steadily in line with the rest of us. It was the way those feathers were rising upwards that shook me most, like each one carried a share of his spirit away from no-man's land. God rest his soul.

It was no time to linger. I could hear and feel my birds moving in the basket on my back so I knew I must press on. The ghost of the wood was soon visible through the mists, rising up from the ridge like ragged tombstones. In the chaos of battle, I was glad simply to follow orders. The sergeant—I forget his name now—told me to stick to him like glue once we made our objective. We pushed forward in waves, with companies leap-frogging one another. Before we knew it, we were in the heart of the wood, the Germans fleeing before us. Our blood was up so, we barely knew what to do with ourselves, but there is always a job for every man. I was asked to send my first bird back with a message that we'd reached our first objective and that we were pressing on towards the second.

We had a look in the German dug-outs. It must have been hell existing in that wood while our heavies shelled them, but to give them credit, those Huns were well-organised and it seemed to me at the time, better off than we were in many ways. I pocketed a sausage from a table and couldn't believe my luck. As we came back to the surface, I turned to that brave sergeant to offer him half, just as he took a sniper's round in the neck and went down in utter silence, a crimson word of thanks fixed on his lips.

Word went round that none of the officers had made it. A sergeant from another company rallied us and said we were to move on to our next objective, a quadrant at the rear of the wood. That's when things started to go pear-shaped. We'd advanced only 100 yards when we were heard incoming shells. They were from our own side and for a second we thought nothing of them until they started exploding round us. I threw myself against the torn and pock-marked trunk of a great oak and made myself as small as I could.

'Send a bloody bird! A bird, man!'

The words reached me between explosions, and I eventually came to my senses. The sergeant dictated a short message describing our location, and with trembling hands I reached into my basket and picked the first bird that came into my hands. I rolled the tiny message tightly and tucked it inside the little metal container before fixing it gently to one of his legs. The little blighter had barely got airborne when shrapnel sliced him in two.

I needn't be told to repeat the exercise, but once again the poor thing only made it twenty yards before falling to the ground in an agony of flapping before becoming still.

I reached into my wicker basket for a third time and my heart skipped a beat when I realised that it was Old Harry. If any were to make it, it would be Harry. I wrote the message again and released him into the air. He rose quickly in a blur of wings like he knew all our lives depended on his good speed. Within moments, he too tumbled in mid-air and came crashing down. I rushed over to him, relieved that he was not yet dead, but found to my horror that his blood was all over my hands. He had lost a leg and some wing feathers but seemed anxious to fly. I admit that I said a short prayer, kissed the back of his head, and let him go.

As far we could tell, Old Harry escaped the carnage of our friendly bombardment and miraculously, about seven minutes later the barrage stopped as abruptly as it had begun. My bird was the hero of the day in our company that morning, and by evening the toast of every Anzac.

III

୬ଚ

'I wanted to come here after the Great War, but one didn't travel much in those days, 'specially if you were an invalid like me. Then Hitler came along didn't he? Didn't stop me thinking about it of course, and I kept cuttings from the papers each November.'

I stood in silence behind my 94-year-old grandad, hands resting on his wheelchair, overcome by the sight. From outside the great arched entrance of the Menin Gate I could just make out the 54,986 names of the missing inscribed on its huge side walls. I was 19 then, in 1993, and we were there together for the 75th anniversary. We had a few hours yet before the main ceremony and the last post scheduled at 8pm, and we had two main objectives.

We found *Pte L Watkins*, without much difficulty as I'd researched before we came which panel bore his inscription.

Grandad held his flatcap on his lap, his hands trembling more than usual. I wasn't sure what to say, and anyway was choked myself.

'He was only a year younger than me,' said Grandad.

I swallowed. He had also been a year younger than I was. I'd heard the phrase 'unimaginable horrors', and at that moment, I gained some sense of the truth for the first time.

'Can we go and see it now?' he asked quietly.

We left the empty echoes of great building behind us, heading towards the centre of Ypres and the elegant spire of St Martin's Cathedral, before swinging right along the bank of the canal.

'This is it,' he said, sooner than I imagined.

A line of skeletal trees rose above us on a raised mound.

'Watkins and I parked the loft here for a night. The town was in ruins then of course, even the cathedral was just a pile.'

I looked across to the bustling Belgium town, struggling to imagine. We left the pavement and I pushed him a few metres across the close-mown grass, so we were a little closer.

'It was like every tree then, just a shattered trunk.'

Back home I'd read about the great sweet chestnut tree; how it not only regrew after the Great War but survived the Second World War when its position on the bank had deterred local people from removing all its branches in fear of damaging nearby homes, even though they were desperate for firewood. The Nazis wouldn't have spared it a second glance.

Grandad's shoulders heaved. I bent over, passing him a tissue. Tears rolled down his cheeks.

'Watkins scavenged for a few branches,' he said a minute later. 'We had a brew. Right here it was, I reckon.'

Beyond the tree's naked fingers and the roof tops of the neat town houses, I spotted a flock of pigeons wheeling round the cathedral spire. A single bird peeled away and started towards us.

With a clatter of wings, the pigeon settled on the top branch of the chestnut.

'What sort of world will you live in I wonder?' he said.

A single grey feather drifted down from the treetop, carried between the branches on lost currents.

'I shall never know,' he added, before I could answer.

I stooped down and picked up the feather and handed it to him.

'Old Harry,' he whispered.

I had no words.

That's when he told me his story.

THE SITTER

INVITATION

S he called out of the blue. Would I come visit and sit for her? I mean, we've not spoken for years, so it was a real surprise to be honest. Last time in fact she'd just moved in and I'd wanted to have a proper conversation about life, the universe, and everything— as you do—but she'd been distracted. Couldn't blame her as she had a lot on her mind at the time. That was before she decided to become some kind of super mother.

I'd gathered since that the moniker 'Super Mother' barely scraped the surface. Her menagerie had become legend in the neighbourhood, if not beyond. Her place was by all accounts literally crawling with life. Don't get me wrong, I'm not averse to some companionship, and have nurtured a wide range of creatures myself over the years, but I'm older now and maybe wiser. Talking of which, if I'd been younger—like a quarter younger—I would have fancied my chances with her, but then, as I say, I'm wiser now. I pride myself in seeing beyond her life force and energy, which are pretty awesome let's be honest, but I also recognise that we're not the slightest bit compatible. That said, I was still drawn to her, wasn't I? At home, I no longer have any dependents, so I can go where I like, when I like. Decision made.

It was quite a trek to get there, I can tell you. Felt like light years away. Most of the way it was so damn monotonous, but some of the places I passed through were stellar. But God, it was a hell of a long way. You know when you embark on an all-nighter and sometimes part of your mind goes somewhere different to the conscious part doing the active work, like into some kind of limitless space? Weird but refreshing at the same time, and then suddenly you snap out of it and wonder how you managed to keep control, how you're still alive. I felt that I spent most of the journey in a vacuum.

They say a change is as good as a rest and when I eventually arrived, I was pretty chilled. Talking of which, compared to my place it actually was refreshingly cool there too. Then I read the welcome letter and all thoughts of a relaxing vacation faded instantly into a distant universe.

WELCOME

༺

Hey Kepler

Thanks so much for agreeing to sit for me, and sorry for the long note. There's quite a lot that I need to explain, but then I think you knew what you were letting yourself in for, didn't you? You may not be able to reach me in an emergency, as I'm not sure that I'll have a signal where I'm going, which is why I've tried to think of everything. I would have said that you could reach out to the neighbours, but on both sides they've been absent for a very long time.

I'll be away for one cycle which is the longest time I've had off in all my years, which is to say longer than I care to remember. I nearly went away once, but I'd hardly turned my back on the place when the freezer started to play up. You wouldn't've believed the damage that a little melt can cause. Another time, I'd got everything all lined up to escape and then a volcano blew. You may have heard about it because it affected everyone here. Sometimes I feel that as I soon as I turn my back, every system, animal, and plant conspire together to create instant chaos. That's my theory anyway.

The fish need to be fed every day, the plants watered, recycling comes regularly, don't forget to put fresh meat out daily, and keep a careful eye on the air conditioning because ... sorry, there's me launching into a haphazard list of instructions without explaining things from the beginning. That's me all over. Right, I'll start again and take you through each task.

Okay, systems first. The air conditioning is a little fickle, to say the least, and it's been playing up a lot recently. I reckon it's been affected by power surges; that or some creature has got inside and unwittingly managed to meddle with it. If I'm really desperate, I resort to resetting it by switching off the power at the board. You must wait for eons before switching everything back on, and if you don't wait long enough then it won't reset properly. The downside is that everything else is affected while the power is down, including refrigeration, aquatic pumps and filters, and of course the place becomes unbearably stuffy.

The freezer is similarly sensitive. I've recently defrosted and restocked it, but it still seems to be continuously thawing. I wonder if the seals are going because whatever I do it doesn't seem to be keeping cold enough. I worry about those things that really must be kept frozen, some of which are pretty unique, and I've not got any contents insurance. Anyway, you'll need to mop the floor otherwise the whole place is likely to flood, then God knows what events that might trigger. As you can imagine, if you need to reset the air con, then this will only get worse.

In the garden there's a series of natural ponds to catch rainwater. You can use these to water the veg garden, and if it's really dry then you can connect a hose and keep everything green. I know the conservatory looks like a forest and you may wonder how you can possibly keep everything watered, but actually it's quite simple as long as no critters, small or large, disrupt the arrangements. I've rigged up an irrigation system which uses the recycled rainwater, and any overflow moves onto the next needy plant. Actually, I'm really proud of the whole set up as it works a treat. I guess a problem could arise if there's a drought, in which case you'll have to draw up water from the aquifer. I've not used the well for a while, and last time I nearly got shafted, so I'd be real careful if you need to use it. Definitely a last resort.

While we're on plants, they occasionally need feeding. There's a bottle of stuff made up in the greenhouse. I use pond weed and droppings collected from the hutches, mixed with a little of my pee watered down with rainwater to make up the concoction. If it runs out, feel free to make your own version. You never know, it may prove better than mine! Occasionally, I add fresh blood from some of the mammals or fish, and sometimes I add ground-up dried fungi. It's amazing how much greener and glossy the leaves become with some regular nutrients. The exotics need to have their leaves wiped free of dust once in a while.

In the drawers under the raised beds you'll find my fungus collection. You won't need to do anything with them, not at this time of year. They get everything they need from the plants above (and *vice versa* of course). It's a good place to put any bodies too, as down there they decompose really efficiently.

To be honest, the fish are among the least demanding as they tend to look after themselves. Even if you don't feed them regularly, they seem to be very self-sufficient, although the smaller fry are likely to disappear! Keep an eye on the water temperature for the tropicals, and the salinity for the marines. In the open water, at this time of year you can leave them to themselves. There's a few predators which take them, mostly birds, but not so many that they cause any noticeable difference.

Let's mention the birds. You never get much back from them emotionally, as I'm sure you know, but you won't be allowed to get away with any lack of care as they'll start up a fearsome racket. I used to clip the wings of the outdoor ones, but they're so well trained now I don't bother. They like to keep an eye on the place, and I swear that they know when something's about to go down. The last volcanic eruption was a good example; they wouldn't settle, like were real flighty in the hours before. You wouldn't believe me if I told you what they did. Anyway, they'll come back to roost every dusk and if they don't ... well, if they don't there's nothing you can do about it, so don't worry.

The insects can be tricky. If numbers get too high, they eventually tend to get sorted out by other insects, or the birds and reptiles. There are just a few whose populations can explode, and then they can disrupt nearly every life-form. To be honest, I've not yet come up with a solution, although in the end things do tend to settle down again. You're not squeamish are you, so I think you'll enjoy relaxing in the conservatory while the larger insects and reptiles are hunting.

Really, it's the mammals that are likely to tax you most, as they can be so wilful. Generally, the more intelligent, the greater the trouble. Some are prone to running amok almost anywhere on the property, and if you're not careful they would happily out compete every other creature with no remorse. There is one in particular—and I think it needs no introduction—that you should watch very carefully. I can honestly say that despite its amazing capabilities, both physical and mental, it is becoming ever more difficult to control. I have resorted to culling some of the worst culprits, though it never brings me any joy, but when they disrupt nearly every system that I've created it is very frustrating. The problem—and I must level with you here—has been getting a lost worse recently, to the extent that I wondered whether I should go away at all. I thought long and hard about it, but eventually came to a difficult decision, and a solution. I'm sorry if this means that it might be you who needs to implement it, but if needs must, you have my blessing.

You will know that these particular creatures are very successful in almost every aspect of life, including reproduction. Their numbers have grown to such an extent that you will find them causing chaos almost everywhere. Luckily for us, but perhaps not for them, they are social creatures which is perhaps their main weakness. I have been nurturing a new pseudo-lifeform which I have tested with great effect on a limited number of hosts with considerable success. The bats have agreed to carry it safely for me while I'm away, but I'm confident that it'll remain out of harm's way. Even the two-legged aren't stupid enough to eat a winged mammal. If for any reason, you find yourself unable to deal with them, have a word with the bats. They know what to do in an emergency.

Best of luck!
G

Emergency tel: 0 15-21-18 13-15-20-8-5-18

CHAOS

༂

When the present determines the future, but the approximate present does not approximately determine the future, that's what I'd call chaos.

She hadn't long departed, and I stood there reading her letter, wondering what I'd let myself in for, when unknown to me everything had already started to unravel. Talk about sensitive systems. Maybe one of the swallowtail butterflies took to the air in a disruptive way in the conservatory, or a drop of power caused the freezer to melt more than usual. More likely it was the humans consuming bats. All I know is that chaos became my realm and in every dominion disturbance reigned. For a long while I feared a mass extinction. In the end ... well, eventually, it was the end for some of them, but they had it coming, let's be honest.

Gaia was nice about it, considering. She told me that the place was older and stronger than its billions of inhabitants which have come and gone over time, but it's back to 452b for me. I'm not sure she'll invite me to sit for her again.

OXBRIDGE
ENVIRONMENTAL
DICTIONARY

2050 EDITION

WONDER

When the worldwide web went AWOL, the whole world wished as one for a reawakening of wisdom, and wept for the wraith of the written word. We—

I t's a short extract but rather extraordinary, don't you think? We're unsure if this was a style at the time or merely a deliberate attempt at wordplay by the writer. What we know without doubt is that it's from a newspaper, whose recycled fibres suggest a North American source commonly used in the 21st century. Given the content, it's likely to be from the late 2060s, possibly early 70s.

'This next one, let me tell you, is something. It's a small fragment but most of the words are there, just the familiar water damage and burnt edges. As you can see it's printed on heavyweight cream paper. Along with the unusual font, the red colour used for the footer is very rare. Overall, given the style and the fact this was on page 356 no less, it all points towards a major literary work which would've required considerable resources to produce. Of course, we don't know the date or who the author was, but whoever she or he was, they loved their trees.'

... to own or manage a forest can surely recognise the burden of ... ... to provide goods and services as well as guardianship and must work with utmost industry to bequeath this resource in a state superior to ... ... inherited. Anyone who has a garden, park or orchard tree has an opportunity to ensure that it offers protection, brings beauty and bears fruit

for future . . .   .   every one of us should aspire to be
a forester.

'Deep isn't it? The words move me every time, I can tell you. I've got that last sentence, the one about aspiring to be a forester, quoted above my door. You may have noticed it when you came in. Anyway, if you look to the right here you can see a separate column of words. They're in italics and also in red which suggests they weren't the main text body but perhaps a caption. You know what that means right? There was at least one illustration in the book. Imagine if we could see it! The meaning remains unclear as only a few words remain legible.'

—of sugi (Crypto—
—grow—

'Enough of these fragments, right? I've saved the best 'til last. I know you've been waiting patiently to see the book, and given that you've walked for twelve days to reach me you're clearly a very committed collector, but first let me tell you the story about how I found it. Would you like that? Of course you would. I'll make us a herb tea.'

OF THE EARTH

༂ᢒ

'No, I'll pass thanks.'

She'd already risen and was heading for a room I assumed she used as the kitchen. She stopped so abruptly she lost her balance. Maybe it was because I finally managed to get a word in edgeways, or perhaps it was my rejection of her herbal infusion. Whatever the reason, it was the first moment she'd let me speak since I'd announced my arrival by shouting up at the house from beyond the giant locked iron gates. 'Oh my, oh my,' she'd repeated over and over as she hurried out of the door and weaved her way through the waist-high weeds of the winding path to welcome me.

Now she studied me in silence, a steely fire in her eyes. She had 20 years on me, her streaked white and grey hair pulled back to a bun pinned haphazardly at the back of her head, exposing the liver spots scattered across her brow which undulated in a deepening frown. Beyond the surprise captured in her slack jaw, for an instant I caught the flash of an altogether different emotion.

'I mean, not yet,' I said, feeling suddenly on edge. Was she alone in the house, what was she toying with in the large pocket of her tatty loose jacket?

'The tea or the story?' she asked, her voice low and measured.

'I'm not thirsty,' I replied quickly, 'but I'd like to hear the story behind your find.'

'Oh sure,' she said, a friendly smile creeping from the corners of her mouth. Her eyes suggested otherwise.

Now was the right time, I decided. 'Actually, I've got something you may like to see.'

'Oh really?'

'I didn't bring much with me, for obvious reasons, and my collection is small compared to yours by all accounts, but I've one of my most precious items to show you. I'd thought you'd find it interesting, but now I realise it'll be something altogether more alluring.'

She came over and sat back down, wrapping her jacket more tightly round herself. I felt a cold breeze reaching my exposed ankles and wondered why she'd not boarded up her windows more effectively. She'd perhaps not used the house for long. The small table between us was scattered with a collection of small boxes but was clean of dust. Under a large magnifying glass lay a scrap of paper crammed edge-to-edge with neat tiny writing. It was the largest piece of paper I'd ever seen, almost two full hand spans across its widest part, with sections of straight edge along no less than three of its sides. It was creased as you'd expect but had been skilfully hot-ironed. Nearby, a dip pen rested by a bottle of ink next to a scrap of blotting rag held safely in place by an open box of shotgun cartridges.

'What do you use?' I asked, pointing to the small glass bottle.

'Mostly gall ink, though it's pretty hard to find any galls, as you know.'

'You should come to Washington state,' I offered. 'There's an ancient oak tree we protect, in a secret location of course. It's the last one alive our side of the Columbia. Last year we recorded our first gall wasps. No galls yet, but we're hoping.'

'I'd like that. In fact, the group's been talking about a touring ecobib exhibition. Maybe we could combine the two.'

She held my gaze.

I nodded and managed a smile.

'Well, what is it?' she asked.

'Sorry?'

'What is it you have with you?'

I reached down to the haversack between my feet. I sensed her watching my every move.

'It's an interesting piece for any bibliophile,' I said, 'but for the likes of us ecobibs, it's special.'

I'd already removed the piece from the tiny hidden compartment sewn under the haversack's base, so I simply reached in and drew it out.

'Oh my, oh—'

'You notice the thick cream paper and the red ink used in the footer?' I said, excited by her reaction.

She went white, her lips moving as if muttering a prayer to François de Sales himself.

'There are only a few words visible, but I'm sure you'll recognise the font straightaway.'

> *— up a tree's vesse—*
> *process called tran—*
> *evaporation of wa—*
> *water through the —*

'May I see for myself?' she uttered, reaching for her magnifying glass.

I hesitated. 'Yes, of course. I think you'll be equally interested in what's next to the text.'

She reached out for the fragment, her hand trembling.

'That's part of a drawing!' she exclaimed, 'I was right!' She cradled the piece delicately in her palm. 'Oh my, how did you come across this?'

'My father actually. He gave it to me when I was seven and I've never looked back as a collector. He taught me to write too.'

'What a treasure.'

'The footer reads page "23" and "Of the Earth". I've always assumed that was a chapter title, not the book's.'

'Yes, I'm sure you're right,' she answered, not taking her eye from the glass. 'That was the convention. On the opposite page may have been the author's name. One day perhaps ...'

She was enraptured. 'When I was a child, I thought they were worms, in the drawing I mean. But now of course I realise they're roots, probably of a seedling, though I've never seen one. I think the text is about the role of roots in taking up water.'

'I guess.'

'So, you agree it's likely to be from the same book?' I asked.

'I'm sure of it, but we can ask the group. We're meeting tomorrow. You could join us. Would you like to stay here?'

It was a rare offer. After all, there's nothing more difficult than finding a safe place to rest in a strange district. 'That's generous of you.' We stared at each other, perhaps both wondering how the balance was settling. 'Can I ask you about the book?' I asked finally.

'Of course. You've been more patient than many others.'

I didn't flinch. She continued to stare. Her eyes followed my every movement as I picked up my precious piece and placed it back in the bag by my feet. 'Is it true, what they say about the book?'

'You can see for yourself; I'll fetch it in a moment.'

'Is it entire?'

She nodded. 'Completely. Every page, every word, every meaning. Even the cover, though it's torn, is in one piece.'

'It's hard to believe,' I said softly.

'Yes, it is.'

'And is it true, about what it says ... how it explains—'

'Oh my. Let's stop talking about it as though it doesn't exist, shall we?' She pushed back her chair. 'I'll fetch it. Wait here.'

'Actually, I think I've changed my mind,' I said quickly.

She paused, hands on the table, halfway to standing.

'I would quite like a tea, if you don't mind?'

She swept a loose bang of silver hair from her eyes. 'Of course,' she replied after the briefest of hesitations.

I had to move fast. As soon as she'd disappeared from sight, I hurried round to her side of the table. Underneath I found a rough scabbard taped to its frame. The hidden blade wasn't an elegant sort, more for slashing that stabbing. I put it in my bag. I moved stealthily towards the open door into the kitchen. I could hear the kettle coming to the boil. The shotgun was leaning against the wall behind the door.

CENSORED

༺

I was on my way back to my seat when she suddenly appeared.

'Shall I g—' She froze, looking first to the steaming mugs in each of her hands, and then to the table now out of reach behind me.

I spoke first. 'It's an unusual word, "wraith", don't you think?'

'What?'

'Wraith, it's unusual,' I repeated.

'Yes, I suppose it is.'

'My father first taught it to me. I remember he had a newspaper cutting which he often read to me. It was a sentence with too many "w" words. One of them was "wraith". He told me it meant spirit or phantom. I wondered how he was so wise, how he could know the meaning of every word in the world.'

'Oh, really?' Circular waves appeared on the surfaces of the teas. She held her ground, but her eyes betrayed her. She glanced right, towards the door.

'Yes, really. He had an even more precious bibliographic treasure. He showed it to me only once, on my tenth birthday. It was a whole book, with bright green and red diagonal stripes cutting across a corner of its shiny blue cover. Inside, every page was present, unblemished and pristine. It seems unreal now, like a dream. He always carried it with him, along with his smaller artefacts, even when he went touring.'

She stared at me, apparently lost for words.

'In fact, the last time I saw him he was setting out for this very state, twenty years ago.'

'Is that so?'

'How did you say you came about the book?' I asked.

Our eyes were locked together.

'How did you know?' she asked, barely audibly.

'You must've heard of your infamous label as the "State Censor"? Where better to hide than among the bibliophiles themselves, a wolf in sheep's clothing, a cuckoo chick among the fledging ecobibs?'

She hurled both mugs at me. I ducked, screaming as scolding tea drenched my back. By the time I'd recovered, she'd reached for the gun behind the door.

It wasn't an evil smile, her expression was caught somewhere between pity and curiosity.

I stopped dead.

She levelled the shotgun and I watched her finger slowly squeeze the trigger.

EVOLUTION

※

She looked less surprised than I'd imagined in the scene that had played out in my mind. The dull click of the trigger, the dawning realisation that I'd removed the cartridges.

As she raised the weight of the impotent gun over her head I charged. Father taught me that attack was preferable to defence, that getting up close gave you an edge, allowing a chance for skill and cunning to win over technology. The tip of my stiletto was twisting inside her heart before she could bring the gun down. He'd've been proud—survival of the fittest he called it.

I wanted to ask her why. I wanted her to tell me who else she'd wasted. I wanted to ask her where, where in this hell hole she'd concealed the wonder of wonders.

She'd departed her lifeless body, without so much as an 'oh my', even before it'd reached the ground.

I wiped the still-keen blade on her jacket.

It took me two days of relentless searching to find and then extract the book.

WORDLESS

❧

When the first human beings watched the azure blue half-sphere of the Earth rise over the Moon they had been awestruck and words had failed them.

I was more excited than those astronauts. My hands trembled as I held the book in front of me, in my own hands. All I could do was stare at it, feeling the weight of its entirety in my arms, its solidity in my grip. Rivulets of tears fell from my eyes.

She'd done a good job, but not good enough. It was hidden under a heavy solid wood bed, underneath a rough weave carpet, below a loose worn floorboard, inside a welded box bolted to the wooden rafters, locked with a weighty padlock.

The book had a shiny dark blue wrapper which I'd heard was called a dust jacket. It was mostly intact, except for a gaping tear on its front, running across to the spine. Above it was the title, spread across several lines in an impressive white font: *Oxbridge Environmental Dictionary, Revised and Updated, Edited by Dr Gabriel Hemery.* In the bottom right corner, in bold red text above two bright angled stripes in green and red, was the precious confirmation: *2050 Edition.* Its dark grey textured cloth boards were visible beneath the torn jacket. The page ends were stained but I could see without opening the book that every one of them was intact.

I went downstairs cradling the unrevealed treasure in both arms. I needed to sit. I needed to savour every moment, and I needed to stem my tears, if only for the book's sake.

I'd been told the entries would be arranged in alphabetical order, so it should've been no surprise to be dazzled by dozens of 'Z's when I opened the book towards its back. There were so many words, so many unfamiliar terms: **zygotaxis**—*mutual attraction between female and male **gametes***; is that what they used to call it? I flicked back a few pages: **xenodeme**—*a deme of **parasites** differing from others in **host** specificity*; sounded like the censors.

I jumped forward to the first few pages, skipping past short 'primer' essays providing context for terms and discursive arguments. The 'A's were absorbing:

> **acidifextinction**—*the mass **extinction** of **organisms** caused by **acidification** in **marine ecosystems**, coined in 2036. First came to the notice of scientists in the late 20th century in the form of **coral bleaching**. The implications for the climate from the loss of coccolithophore ... Then* **acidification (ocean)**, **adaptation**, **afforestation**, **albedo**, *and the* **Alvarez hypothesis**. *The* **Amery ice shelf**—*a large ice shelf on the east coast of Antarctica which first came to public prominence in 2019 when it calved an iceberg known as D-28 which was twice the size of New York City. Its rapid retreat, shrinking 80km by 2048, has since made it a focus for international public concern linked to the **climate catastrophe**.*

That was my cue. No more prevarication. I turned a bundle of leaves forward, landing on **cladogenesis**. My fingers trembled. Another page or two:

> **climate**, **climacteric**, **climatype**. *At last:* **climate change**—*first described in the 1950s when the theory of **global warming** was proposed by scientists, later labelled **climate crisis** and then **climate emergency** in the 2010s, formally termed the **climate catastrophe** in 2026 by the United Nations Convention of Parties COP32. Finally, there it was:* **climate extinction**—*the mass complete disappearance of*

*species caused by **anthropogenic** activities after a series of **tipping points** led to a **global cascade**—*

EXTERMINATED

That was it. That's all we found of my mother's notes, tucked into a tiny pocket hidden in the base of her otherwise empty haversack, dumped next to her wasting body by the wayside.

Her tiny writing was so compact that each line nudged the line above, her lower loops caressing the words waiting to be written. The scrap of paper had given up all of its white in the fight against the censor. Most likely, my mother had been searching for another sheet of paper to continue her notes.

I've never stopped looking, not in the fifty years since. As long as our species remains extant and zygotaxis exists, our search for the truth will continue across generations.

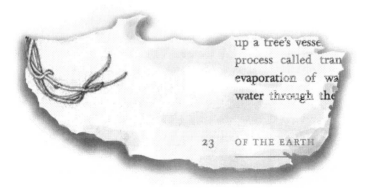

up a tree's vesse
process called tran
evaporation of wa
water through the

23   OF THE EARTH

QUERCUS

DECEM

༄

TEN

Oh, eyeful of wonder
I am not blind to you

I'd never seen one before, at least not outside of a book. Maybe it's because I'm 10 years old and much better at looking. The summer tourist perched on the tip of the oak tree's lowest branch, perfectly hidden among the dappled shadows of its spring leaves and dangling green flowers, like a feathered zebra. The male pied flycatcher only betrayed its position each time it rose to catch an unsuspecting insect, flying in a dizzying acrobatic loop. I watched him through my binoculars for 20 minutes as he fed greedily on mayflies rising from the damp grass. I drew some pictures of him in my field notebook. I was disappointed that I didn't need to use my new crayons because he was only black and white, so I drew some green-lobed oak leaves. Then I had the great idea of drawing a small tortoiseshell butterfly that my flycatcher was about to dart out and eat, and I used every colour except pink.

It was a good drawing, I decided. I looked back to the tree's spreading crown and my eyes travelled down its massive trunk through my binoculars. I caught the tail-end of a nuthatch as it disappeared from view behind the trunk, scurrying across the rough bark, only for it to reappear round the other side as a treecreeper. I giggled at the pair's magic trick.

I remembered Mum's sandwiches and my stomach rumbled. I'd been out since the dawn chorus had begun and it must be lunchtime by now. I raised my arm to look at my watch but admired my home-knitted jumper instead. The thick cable knit turtleneck was mottled green and brown because I'd asked her to knit me a camouflage jumper for Christmas last year. The winter of 1976 was very cold, and it followed the driest summer that even Mum and Dad say they've ever seen. I had to share the bathwater with my sister, and we only flushed the loo after a number two.

'My dear boy, that's a sacred ibis!' is what H G Hurrell said to me when Dad and I dropped in on him last summer, soon after the first rain fell. A month before I'd visited the local nature reserve on a school trip and sketched it because it was the first bird I'd ever seen that I couldn't identify. It was not in any of my books. I knew that it wasn't, but when I got home from boarding school weeks later, I'd checked, just in case. As a reward for the rare sighting and my sketch, which he said was really good, Mr Hurrell had gifted me his copy of Eric Hosking's memoire, *An Eye for a Bird*, signed by the author himself. It's the best title ever because it means two things; it's about the bird photographer's life and how he lost an eye to a tawny owl. The book is on my most important shelf lined up with my other bird books which altogether take up three shelves in my bedroom.

Brushing moss and discarded oak flowers off my woolly sleeve, I peered through the scratched and cracked glass of my Timex. Half past ten, that can't be right! Stuff it, I'll eat anyway.

I stomped over to the oak tree. I realised it was bigger than I'd thought. It wasn't the tallest tree around, there were much taller ones in the nearby woodland, but out here on its own in the middle of the meadow, its leafy canopy was twice the width of other trees. And then there was its trunk which was enormous. I reckoned it wouldn't fit in my bedroom, so I measured it with my arms. With my arms stretched their widest it was seven-and-a-bit times around. I started to work out the maths, because Dad told me my arm span was the same as my height which is 1.40m. That means I should be able to work it out ... 7 x 1m, plus 7 x 40cm which is 280cm, which adds up to 9.8m plus the bit I didn't measure ... let's say 10m. Maybe more. Man, I was hungry.

'Sorry,' I said to the great tit overhead, who was shouting in alarm as I sat down and leaned against the trunk of her oak tree. I unwrapped the greaseproof paper from a stack of four sliced-white sandwiches, filled with grated cheddar and oozing with homemade pickle. It was the first time that year that I could feel the heat of the sun on my face, and I was out of the cool breeze on this side of the tree. Two sandwiches in, I peeled off my jumper and placed it behind my head. My neck was sweaty and itched against the scratchy wool. The tree's rough bark hurt my head because I'd just had a haircut and could feel every ridge and crenulation. Dad said that the top of castle walls are crenellated. I like "C" words. My other favourite word is crepuscular, which means that you like dawn and dusk. I think I'm crepuscular, but I'm usually tired after my supper, so maybe I'm half crepuscular. The woodcock is crepuscular ... it can see 360° degrees around all at once ... and ...

A curious mixed scent of earth and lanolin greeted me. My left arm had been stretched out before me, under my jumper, cushioning my head from the ground. It was so dead; I'd lost all feeling in it. Terrified, I opened my eyes to check if it was still there. My favourite left arm was there alright, but I could only see, not feel, its fingers clenched rigidly like claws. They disappeared inside a bark crevice along one of the buttress roots. Rigor mortis had set in.

When Ginger had died, Dad had taken a long time to dig a hole in the garden. I'd wrapped him up in my old red jumper that we'd found him stretched out in that morning. He hadn't come for his Kitbits. He never missed his breakfast biscuits, and always came running when I called his name. I could call him best because I had the highest voice; that's one of the benefits of being a trained chorister. He'd come through the cat flap miaowing loudly, his orange tail waving from side-to-side. Dad's hole wasn't big enough and we couldn't curl him up tight enough to fit in. Mum said he was too stiff. Dad said it was rigor mortis which I'd never heard of before. Ginger stayed in my red jumper all that day and night, but we buried him next morning when we were sure he'd fit in the ground. Mum said he would like to be buried curled up. Dad was grumpy. I think he'd hurt his back digging the hole.

For a second I wondered if Dad could dig a hole big enough for my arm, before I told myself I was being silly. I reached round with my good arm and pared my dead fingers away from the tree, lifting the arm which was once my friend. It was so weird, like I was touching and holding someone else's limb. I felt warm blood pouring into it before the worst pins and needles ever erupted in my fingers and spread up my arm. I cried, but no one could see me, so that was okay.

I wiped my eyes, and ran my fingers tips over my cheeks, fascinated by the weird cable knit indentations in my skin before they faded. Using the back of my hand, I removed the dribble from the side of my mouth and raised my head to look around. A steamroller had flattened my two remaining sandwiches. Cheese matter lay splattered round me in the leaf litter, and pickle oozed from the brown waxy paper. The remains looked like the many myxomatosis casualties up and down our lane after the poor rabbits had sought and received merciful relief, usually courtesy of our neighbour's Ford Cortina. A colony of emergency ant services were already clearing the cheesy scene.

I rolled sleepily onto my back and gazed up into the waving leaves. I squinted at the dazzling midday sun flickering through the canopy. Then I remembered my wonderful dreams. The tree had told me a story about the beginning of life, long before I and even he had been born; older than time itself. In a second dream, I had told a story in return, and it was as real as anything. I had a powerful birdwatching scope and had the luck of spotting an eagle owl here in England. I could still feel the excitement and how it led me on a dizzying journey through the web of life. Most thrilling of all, I was a grown up. I'd felt what it was like, to be able to do things by myself, to know more things. I didn't really understand the tree's story though, it was weird. I've heard the bible version of the creation so many times. There's a picture of Adam and Eve in *Genesis* in my bible, the one that Dad gave me when I went to choir school. It says 'To our loving Son' inside. He wrote it using his best fountain pen, which he uses for signing important things, but he wrote 'Daddy and Mummy' below the message in my bible. I like that it has a green shiny cover with the crossed keys symbol of the cathedral embossed in gold. Most of the other boys have a red one which matches our scarlet cassocks.

I was 12 the next time something strange happened with my tree. I was home from boarding school for an extra-long summer holiday because I'm always away from home for Christmas and Easter, singing in the cathedral.

Soon after I got home, Dad started behaving strangely. He asked me if I had hair down there—you know—and I said yes, but I was embarrassed. Last time he was weird, he had asked me if white stuff sometimes came out from mine, then he asked me to go to the bathroom and make some come out into a plastic bag he gave me. I was confused because it had only come out twice, and both times I'd been asleep when it'd happened. He looked disappointed when I gave him back the bag, empty, 10 minutes later.

This morning, Mum and Dad had a really big argument. It was something to do with Sis, because I heard Mum saying her name really loud, lots of times. She's 14 now and has become really grumpy, and has been shouting at all of us—a lot. She didn't hear them quarrel because she's not at home. She went to stay with Nan last week, and she's not come back yet.

I went to my favourite tree to escape the shouting. I make my own sandwiches now. Peanut butter with iceberg lettuce is my favourite. I found some cold roast potatoes in the fridge, next to the leftover chicken which I was looking for, so I brought three of them too. Mum tosses roasties in mustard powder and salt, which makes them really crispy. I placed the remains of the chicken 50 paces away and tethered it to a hazel peg with a bit of string, and then waited patiently with binoculars in hand, leaning back against the oak.

Immediately behind the chicken bones was the carcass of a huge elm. It was killed by DED—that's Dutch elm disease. Its trunk was really big, about 7m around, which my favourite tree book says means it's 700 years old. Well, it was, but now it's dead. It died two years ago. There are two smaller elm trees that I spotted in the distance through my binoculars before I watched a common buzzard land on the tallest dead branch of Elvis. That's the elm's name because he died the same year as the famous rock star, but Elvis—the American Elvis—was only 42. My Elvis was 16-and-something remainder times older than him, but not famous at all. Only I know much about my Elvis. I looked up 1277, his birth year, in Encyclopaedia Brittanica and it says it was the first time the St George Cross was used for our flag and when Edward I was King of England. Elvis lived through so many wars, only to be killed by a disease carried by a beetle. I wondered what will kill me.

The buzzard jumped hard from Elvis' skeleton and I watched it wobble, waving her a slow goodbye as the hawk folded back her wings and dropped into a death-defying swoop towards the chicken. I felt guilty when she face-planted into the long meadow grass and tumbled onto her back. I hadn't expected any bird to grab it in mid-flight. Shaking her head, she recovered her composure and jumped onto the carcass, spreading her wings to cover it just like the vultures that I watched on Life on Earth last week. It's my favourite programme ever, way better than Blue Peter.

I daren't move while she stripped the remaining meat from the carcass, but after she flew back to Elvis I watched through my binoculars as she wiped her greasy beak against his dry ribs. She closed her eyes and looked satisfied. I put down my binoculars and tucked into my lunch, and watched as three carrion crows landed one after the other and began to squabble over the chicken bones. A robin took the crusts that I threw in front of my feet. It wasn't afraid of me.

Oak is old. That's his name. Nothing showy like Elvis, just Oak. Last time I was here, I brought enough string to reach right round his trunk, and when I got home I measured it. It was 10.12m, which means he's definitely more than 1,000 years old. I think he's the oldest tree in the world. I'm the only one who knows about him. It's our secret.

There must have been peanut butter left on the crust because the robin spent ages wiping his beak on the ground. I wondered what may come along and pick the peanut butter from the grass stems or lick the chicken grease from the dead elm wood. I'd created two new food chains. I was the peanut butter god, giving life to all. An old dream that Oak once told me drifted back into my mind; a story about the beginning of life and the Tree Commandments dictated by Mother Gaia. I remembered waking up confused and sweating under the great tree. I'd so loved that green woolly jumper, even though it made me itch. It's the dog's bed now, although our kitten likes to lie on it if she can.

I reached behind with both arms, feeling for good handholds in Oak's furrowed bark. I felt as though we were a team facing out towards the world together. The bark held fast as I pulled my back hard against him, unlike the poor elm tree. Last week, I'd easily peeled away some of Elvis' skin with my Swiss army knife and discovered huge feeding galleries left behind by *Scolytus scolytus*. That's the first Latin name I've ever remembered for an insect. I hope there's never a thing like French Oak Fungus or Spanish Oak Sickness.

Last term, Mrs Green, our history teacher, taught us about Nazi concentration camps. She didn't tell us about the medical experiments that they did on the Jews. I read about that in Brittanica when I got home. I wondered if Dad was a Nazi, but then I felt bad. Charlie and I have showed each other our things, and I even touched his once, after lights out. It was exciting because I knew it was naughty. With Dad it was different; I was scared.

The robin returned, looking for more crusts, but I'd none left. I threw him a juicy green caterpillar that was looping across my boot, then I felt guilty because it might have grown into a purple emperor. I wondered if Gaia ever felt guilty.

Oak might be the oldest tree in the world. He felt like it under my fingers. I'll look it up in Brittanica. It might be under 'age' or 'plants', if I can't find it under 'trees'. His birth year—or is it his seed year—must be 979, although he might be older? I don't know what happened in 979, but he was alive for the Battle of Hastings in 1066. He was ... 87 years old ... which is older than I may ever be. I wonder what happened in 1155, 1244, 1333 ...? I'll look it up in ...

I woke, blinking at the golden sun which had dipped below the fringes of Oak's swaying branches.

Jeez, I'm wearing a yellow and white checked dress ... I'm a girl, but I don't even know my own name ...

Duh, that's the tea towel I wrapped my lunch in!

It had happened again; two more weird dreams. The only time I'd ever dreamed like that before was when I'd fallen asleep against Oak when I was 10 years old.

Was it a coincidence that one of the dreams was of trees and Nazis? I liked the girl in the dream; she'd be a cool friend. I bet it was like a holiday, escaping from London to the country during the war. I would miss Mum though. The long terms at school are bad enough. I hate headmaster Mr Petts. Last term, he was angry because I spoke to Mum and Dad when they'd come all the way to the cathedral on a Sunday morning to listen to me sing a solo. He interrupted us talking after the service, saying I had to go back to the school. As soon as Mum and Dad left, he started shouting at me, then he grabbed my hair really hard and dragged me like that the whole way across the cathedral close back to school. It was far enough that my head was numb by the time we reached it, so I was relieved my friends didn't see me crying. It must have looked strange to the tourists and locals; a boy in a red cassock being marched roughly that way, but no one said anything. Maybe they thought it was the way choristers were persuaded to sing for their pleasure three times a day.

The second dream featured tree terrorists returning an ancient bonsai to the wild. I'd really love to go to Japan, but I'm not so sure about earthquakes. I did run away from school once, but it was after dark and no-one noticed I'd even gone when I climbed back up the fire escape to the dorm and crept back into my bed. I was like a ninja, or was it a shinobi?

I stood up, stretching my legs, then leaned against Oak and hugged him. I closed my eyes and thanked him for making me feel good. In return, he hit me on the head, at least I think he made it happen. I looked up and there was a jay hopping about in his top branches, swearing at me. 'Spaz, spaz-spaz,' she shouted. I picked up her missile from between my feet. I studied the alien acorn. Only a tiny part of its normally-smooth shell was visible, most of it was covered with weird ridges and crests. I put it in my safest pocket to look up later, next to my fold-up 10x21 field lens and my Swiss army knife on its cord lanyard.

I packed up my things and gave Oak another hug. Stretching on my tiptoes, I could just reach a great swirling eye of bark below his craggy frown. I felt a tingle when I ran my fingers over it. I don't want the holidays to end, but next year will be my last as a chorister. My best friend Tom's voice has already broken, and he's now singing in the back row as a tenor. I don't like that he shows off that he's with the men. He's started shaving too, but we tease him about the bum fluff on his top lip. We'll start practising the *Miserere mei, Deus* soon. All the boys can reach top A, but only three of us could sing C6 really well last year. The choirmaster Mr Dundall couldn't believe that I could actually reach top G, five notes above C6. He says that I'll solo Psalm 50 next time. Dad says that when I sing the *Miserere* all the hairs on his neck and arms stand up. It used to make me more nervous than singing *Once in Royal David's City* to a packed cathedral on Christmas eve. Now that I'm 12 I'm used to it because I've sung the *Miserere* every year since I left home and joined the choir, which is now exactly four years ago.

As I left the meadow, I turned back for a last look at Oak, wondering if he could see my little figure through his hidden eye. He held a glowing ball of fire in his branches, and sunlight flared out in every direction, just like Japan's rising sun flag except that this was yellow ... and of course the sun was falling not rising.

His mighty shadow reached out to touch my feet planted between the bladder campion and scarlet pimpernel.

I didn't know it then, but as I turned for home, deeply happy, it was the last time I'd see him with a child's eyes.

Andricus quercuscalicis is its Latin name, the gall wasp that produces the knopper gall. One-two, and, three | one-two, three | one-two-three . . .

The Knopper Gall Wasp

Andricus quercuscalicis

Sis turns round and gives me a funny look as I tap out the rhythm on my knees which are pressed hard up against the back of Mum's seat. Music always helps with long words. I hum quietly, but Sis can't hear because her ears are covered with the orange sponge of her Walkman headphones, while Mum is concentrating on the road. The rain's coming down so hard it's bouncing off the tarmac and hammering on the bonnet. The wipers are going so fast I reckon they'll fall off in a minute while the serious debate on Radio 4 is unintelligible.

My voice has broken now. I was an alto for half of last year, but now I can sing tenor and bass. I'm a baritone really because I can't reach the really low notes, although my bottom D's not too bad.

The rain has turned into ice, gathering like snow where the wipers can't reach. I'm scared that the hail will get so big it'll break the windscreen.

I feel for Oak's weird crenellated acorn that I've carried in my pocket ever since we left home, real home that is, two years ago. And, now we're heading back, and I can't wait to see Oak again. Dad might have been a bastard, but he did leave the house to Mum and us when he died, so that's something. The removals van departed before us this morning, but Mum and Sis keep stopping for a pee every hour at one motorway service station after another, so it's taking forever to get there. The men will have unpacked before we arrive.

Fecund. It sounds like a dirty word. The knopper gall wasp lays her eggs in the buds of pedunculate oak, and the growing grubs secrete chemicals which mutate the tree's seed-growing cells. The more grubs, the more of the horny crenellated growths will appear on the surface of the acorn. 'An oak tree's fecundity can be severely affected.' That's what my book said. One creature's fecundity reduces another. The death of one creature, will benefit many others. Dust to dust, ashes to ashes, oaks to oaks.

❦

I'd not gone straight to him. I noticed the negative space first. Mr Hopkins is always on about it in art, telling us we should learn to see the things that others don't, to observe the in-between, to see form in the fabric of nothing which links the something. He has an angry white scar under his right ear where his rifle once backfired. Everyone knows that he used to be a champion marksman. When the twats who don't want to be in his class start whistling, or drag their stools screeching across the parquet floor, he has to cover his ear. When they do it, he's frozen in pain, but afterwards he goes ape, like really ape. Stuart was banned from his classes and has a whole term of extra dining room duties. I'd like to give up music and do art for A-level, but I don't know if I'll be allowed because of my music scholarship. I'm one of only two boys in the whole school who sings or plays any instruments seriously.

It was Elvis, or more accurately the Not-Elvis, which first caught my attention. As I entered the meadow there was a gaping void in the familiar landscape, its fabric rent asunder. Oak was there in the distance, which was a relief. My attention returned to the space between, to the not rather than the is. There was blue sky and unshadowed meadow grass where Elvis' skeleton once stood as gatekeeper to the meadow. A single white cloud hovered above the void for a circling buzzard to loiter on.

Only Elvis' giant stump remained. I said I was sorry as I stepped on him. I could see the scars of a chainsaw stretching across the dark wood in a fan-like pattern. A fistful of little slimy fungi bodies nestled between the remains of two of his buttress roots. The farmer must have cut him down; probably for firewood. I sat on his dry lifeless form for the first time. I reckoned he'll be here for decades. My tree book says that the Romans used elm for drains and water troughs, and its timber is one of the best woods to use outdoors.

Oak gazed imperiously back towards me across the meadow. He'd lost a branch; a big branch. There was a gap in the side of his leafy canopy, and among the shadows was an even darker hollow. I raised my binoculars. His heart was exposed and from the hollow in his trunk the heavy-billed face of a raven stared back at me, blacker than black, glinting in the darkness. My heart thumped. Elvis steadied me.

'Prrk-prrk,' shouted the raven as I approached, before disappearing through the back of Oak in a noisy flurry of wings and scattering leaves.

The hollow in Oak's trunk was difficult to see from the ground, but a bright gash was visible where a huge branch had once reached out. It was a recent wound. The summer storm a few weeks before would have been a severe challenge for him, unable to reduce his sail area in the face of the gale. As for the lost limb, there was none to be seen, but tell-tale piles of chainsaw dust peppered the flattened sheep's fescue. More firewood for the farm.

I reached out with both hands and pressed them against his familiar corky bark. As I shuffled closer with my feet, I crunched a carpet of hollow misshaped acorns. 'You've had more knopper gall wasps visiting,' I said out loud.

They do me little harm, so long as I have plenty of healthy seeds.

'It's that foreign cousin of yours, the turkey oak, which harbours the wasps for the rest of the year. Three hundred years ago, you didn't have to contend with them did you?'

That is man for you. Always interfering.

'I've been away.'

I have not.

'Ha!' I shuffled down to sit with my back against him. Comfortable in his familiar embrace, I looked back across the meadow. Ripples ran through the drying grass flowers, bobbing and curtseying against the spent bladder campion and ox-eye daisy heads. Elvis's stump was invisible. At least the worst of my hay-fever was behind me. That was one advantage while we lived on the estate for the last two summers; I'd hardly suffered at all.

What have you been suffering?

'Hay-fever. Sod's law, that nature threw that at me.'

Is that everything?

'A childhood of extremes, healed only by nature. Isn't that perverse?'

And . . ?

'My dad died.'

Do you suffer still?

'No.'

I think you must be a good son for your mother.

Quinquaginta

༆

Fifty

Through the artful eye may be best to capture,
The hearts of oak and man.

'I met some fish once.'

I wondered how this could possibly be true for a tree growing at the centre of an expansive grassy meadow.

'They fell from above in a summer storm, many, many years ago. They had beautiful coloured sides reflecting in pinks and greens the rays of the sun which shone from the ominously dark clouds that moments earlier had dropped them without warning. For several minutes their eyes stared up at me unblinking from a layer of giant white hail stones. Then the crows came, and they saw no more.'

'I've heard that can happen, but I've never seen it,' I said. 'We have a saying, "it's raining cats and dogs," but I don't reckon it's ever actually happened.'

'The thought of dogs landing on me is enough to make me weep. It is bad enough having them water my feet!'

'They were probably rainbow—'

'Yes, there was a great double one as the storm passed.'

'No, the fish; I think they must've been rainbow trout.' I chuckled at Oak's confusion, wondering why we were talking about fish in the first place.

༈

'It has been a long time,' he said finally, his words whistling through his naked branches before being whipped away by the bitter wind.

I huddled on the lee, close to his side. 'Thirty-four summers and 33 winters,' I replied, thinking it was like we'd never been apart, that the conversation continued from where it had left off though I couldn't remember talking about fish with him before. I tucked my hands deeper into the lined pockets of my dark-green woollen ranger coat and stamped my feet.

'Do you mind!'

'I'm sorry, but it's freezing.' I looked out over the exposed meadow. The tips of the wind-bent grass were dusted with an icing of hoar-frost. A solitary crow rushed silently overhead, allowing itself to be buffeted sideways. The sky was a uniform grey, merging with the hazy silhouettes of the distant forest edge. It seemed unlikely that the sun would make an appearance.

'Are you finding some success with your life?'

'I suppose that I am. I'm happy, and lucky to be doing what I love.'

'What exactly are you doing?' he asked.

'I work with trees.'

'And I think that you have 50 years now.'

'Yes, and you have aged another 40 years since we first met and that means you have one thousand and forty years. You wear your years ever more lightly, at least you do numerically.'

I wondered whether I should share my shock at how much he had physically aged in recent years. His crown had noticeably retrenched, more branches had fallen away, new hollows opened to expose his heart. One at his base was now large enough to conceal a man. The speed of his ageing seemed disproportionate.

'I may be ancient in your time, but I am healthy,' he said, reading my mind.

'There is a new disease killing ash trees. I wrote a scientific paper about it recently. A group of us calculated that it will cost the UK £15 billion. We estimate that 150 million ash trees will die over the next few years.'

'Then us oak trees are lucky indeed. In your lifetime, you have lost first elm, then ash, perhaps others?'

'I don't need reminding.'

Nearby a wren chattered a warning. A large dog fox came into view, trotting across the meadow, lifting its paws daintily over the frozen tips of the long grass. Behind him a mute pink glow kissed the grey eastern horizon.

'What is the real reason you are here, Gabriel?'

I hesitated. 'You know, I admire those who stand, march, and chain themselves to protest at environmental injustices. Instead, I guess I resort to science and writing to fight my battles.'

'I am sure there is virtue in that.'

'I've never shouted on the streets for the cause that I most believe in. I've never been arrested. Do you think I'm a coward?' I asked.

The wren fell silent, and in the distance a green woodpecker laughed. I was unsure which of the two responses Oak might endorse, so I filled the void. 'Maybe I should call myself something heroic, like "Gabriel Forestrider". I can picture myself wielding my evidence sabre and shouting, "may the truth be with you!"'

'Have you won any battles, do you wear any crow feathers among the braids in your hair?'

'I have the scalp of government from 2010!'

'How so?'

'I helped stop it selling off the people's forests.'

'Then indeed you are brave. And what is your new cause?'

'To save you Oak. You're in the frontline against the blitzkrieg of progress and now totally exposed.

Oak remained silent.

'I somehow knew one day that this would happen,' I croaked, swallowing past the tensing lump in my throat.

Overhead, a branch creaked loudly as a fearsome gust of wind rushed past us, shaking free a clutch of dead twigs which fell round me scattering fragments of azure-blue eggshells. Across the meadow a million pink-hued crystals tinkled in the frozen grass.

'Tell me about the enemy, Gabriel Forestrider.'

※

'In the early morning I often have my most creative thoughts. They go round and round in my mind until they gain some sense of reality or purpose.'

I knew that Oak listened, though he said nothing.

'This morning I lay in bed thinking of the wooden trick of the Trojan horse that Odysseus and his fellow Greeks used in the fall of Troy. I don't even know why it was in my head in the first place. Before long the story had been contorted in my mind: Earth was the bastion in place of Troy, our foe was the climate crisis rather than the Greeks, and the world's forests were the Trojan Horse. Even now, I'm not sure it—'

'What, Gabriel? You are unsure of your own twisted mind?'

'Maybe not, but I could have a stratagem of my own to rival Odysseus.'

'Really. How so?'

'After our last chat, I decided to take a stand. "Fucking tree hugger!" That's what a security guard shouted at me the other day when I was protesting at a woodland site destined to be bulldozed.'

'Well, that would be accurate in my experience.'

'Well, yes, and that's exactly it. I am a tree hugger. That's what I'm good at. That's what we do when we're together, and when we're together, we are stronger.'

'I am not following you.'

'You can be a living Trojan Horse, and I can be the enemy within.'

'That doesn't make any sense ... What are you doing?'

'After I last saw you, everything came together in my mind. I'm measuring you. Do you know, I think this might just work.'

'If you say so. You are the silvologist after all.'

'This is hardly silvology,' I answered, putting the tape measure and notebook away in my rucksack and removing my secateurs. 'I hope you don't mind, but I'd like to take a few cuttings from the tips of your most vigorous central branches. It's the perfect time of the year for clonal propagation.'

I worked in silence, my thoughts racing, possibilities running wild. My collection complete, I bade my friend farewell with a promise to return within the month, though I feared it might need to be sooner. I would have to hurry to be ready in time.

'You have still not told me what it is that you have placed at the entrance to my hollow heart?'

Oak's question raised me from a shallow fitful sleep and a wonder of childhood dreams. Immediately alert, I strained to hear the enemy. It was quiet; too quiet. There was no sound of revving engines, nor the stamping feet of massed forces. The full darkness outside had been replaced by a dimpsy grey, yet no headlights pierced the gloom. Still, I felt uneasy and I knew Oak had spoken to me not just to satisfy his curiosity. I held my breath and listened again. There! I could hear footsteps, not far off. Perhaps just a couple of people, making their way slowly towards us. A few indistinguishable words, quietly spoken, drifted towards us.

I sat up stiffly and looked out across the meadow. The bodies behind the sounds approached stealthily from our blind side, hidden from me by the bulk of Oak's remaining trunk. I could hear a muted conversation and caught a few words.

'... are you running?'

Bright artificial light suddenly cast unforgiving shadows and two pairs of feet appeared. Both were clad in brand new walking boots; the sort that no-one who actually rambled or climbed in would ever wear. Nadders' camouflage.

'Professor, are you in there?' asked a soulful female voice while the camera spotlight moved inexorably towards me.

I readied myself.

'Professor ... may I call you Gabriel?'

'Hello,' I answered. 'Yes, I'm here.' I shielded my eyes from the dazzling brightness.

'Channel 4 News. Could we record an interview with you?' The closest pair of boot heels lifted and two sharp blue denim-clad knees lowered in front of me. Long locks of dark wavy hair tumbled into view, swiftly hooked back by an elegant silver-ringed finger to reveal a beautiful smiling face. The reporter reminded me of an Ethiopian colleague from the distant past, and a brief memory of fieldwork in the tropics flashed in my mind.

'Yes, of course. I know why you're here.'

'Would you like to speak with us out here?'

'No, I think I'll remain here, thank you.'

'Of course. Then we'll conduct the interview with you inside the tree. The camera's rolling. Jim, can you get in closer so you can move from me to focus on the professor?'

I waited while they shuffled round each other, moistening my lips in readiness. I listened as they made their final adjustments, and my interviewer cleared her voice. I moved closer to the barred entrance, removed my woollen hat, swept my hand over my hair just in case, and sat upright within my Trojan hollow.

'I have never heard of composite ballistic nano-cellulose.'

Oak and I were alone again as our visitors moved on to take the required filler shots. I watched the pair wander across the meadow, deciding where to set up the tripod for the next shot. My interviewer was speaking into her mobile. Judging from her circling free arm, it was an animated conversation. Eventually, it looked like they were going to choose the stump of Elvis as their platform, and their long shadows stretched out over the waving grass.

'Is it true that the shield you have made is indestructible?' Oak asked.

'Almost, at least not without resorting to heavy cutting equipment which would endanger me.'

'I was surprised she did not ask you more questions about it. Where did you find such a material?'

'From a friend in the New World.'

'There's a new world?'

'Well there was, but no more. It's dying faster than anywhere else on Earth, led towards destruction by an egotist megalomaniac.'

Why?

'Because he rejected any efforts to avoid the climate crisis, even denied the science by—'

'No, I mean why was such a person chosen as their leader?'

'Good question.'

'And why does he care so little for his land and its creatures?'

'I suspect that he suffers from NADD.'

'You should gift him a seed.'

'He would eat it.'

Our visitors were packing away. A glance at a watch, a gesticulation back towards the way they'd come. They were the advance party, I knew that. Tipped off by another of my friends. We had little peacetime remaining. A robin—nature's best-disguised hooligan—struck up a chant nearby. Feeling a chill, I pulled my hat back on.

'Do you think it true, Gabriel, that there is a stand-off beyond the meadow?'

'It'd explain why we've had so few visitors.'

'Your army must be large in number to have halted the piston caterpillars.'

'I wish I could see them.'

'But they have your orders which they must be following.'

'It's not my orders they follow, but a collective conscience. We're a movement of many, acting for a common good. Like wood ants.'

'And what about you, Gabriel? You said you would stay here until the war was won. You told the interviewer that you will use your own hunger to fight this battle. It seems to me to be too great a sacrifice.'

'I'd go to the ends of the Earth for you.'

'I wish I could sustain you in return.'

My eyes welled up, and I swallowed with effort. 'You've always protected me.'

Oak was silent for a moment. 'While there is a lull,' he said finally, 'you should rest.'

⁂

'You realise that you'd enjoy a longer life without humans my friend, yet without you and your companions, my life and the lives of every other animal on Earth would simply cease to be.'

'Is that really so?' asked Oak.

'It's ironic that you aren't aware of how life revolves around you, but I guess there's no reason you should be. Amensal—living together as unlikely dependent organisms where one is unaffected if the other is harmed—that's how trees and people relate. We have an amensal relationship.'

'I think you mistake me for one of your students!'

'It's interesting though, don't you think? Humans exhibit a form of destructive amensalism; a form of antibiosis. So do walnut trees which exude a chemical called juglone from their roots with antibiotic properties, being capable of controlling competing plants—'

'Must every one of our discussions come back to walnuts?'

'You have me there. But here's the irony; humans are troubled by the increasing resilience of bacteria to our antibiotic drugs, but largely oblivious that we ourselves are also antibiotic organisms.'

'So, *Homo sapiens* is an unlikely dependent organism?'

'We're very highly dependent, despite our arrogant dominance over nature. It seems that our intellect has little capacity to recognise this. We seem incapable of living our lives more by symbiosis than antibiosis.'

'You and I are symbiotic right now.'

'Yes, we really are, aren't we? Although from outside, it may appear as though I'm a giant parasite, and that you've ingested me.' As I said the words, a vivid picture of us together formed in my mind, like the scene from a reverse Alien-like sci-fi plot.

'Are they returning?' he asked.

It took a moment to clear my mind of the image. 'I don't know,' I answered finally. It was the truth; I really had no idea. Since the running pitched battles had ended with a mutual staged withdrawal, it had been eerily quiet.

'If you were to die now, you would biodegrade and feed my roots. That would be truly symbiotic.'

'It's so dry in here, I would become a mummy instead.'

'That cannot be Gabriel, for you are a daddy, are you not?'

'You're the best deadpan comedian, and you don't ev—'

The tears welled up suddenly, catching me completely by surprise. I'd been so focussed on my friend and on my mission, I'd hardly spared a thought for my own family. Where were they, what were they doing? Maybe they were watching coverage on TV, or somewhere nearby yet unable to reach me. I felt their anxiety, and the awareness of my selfishness overcame me. I began to sob uncontrollably.

A wild animal howled next to me. Then I recognised it as my own pain. With difficulty I found some focus and managed to calm myself.

Oak remained impassively silent. Outside, fingers of mist spread through the meadow and the bare crowns of the distant forest trees passed a golden torch slowly between them, raising it from the earth and urging it skyward.

༃

'May I be honest, Gabriel? Truly, I did not believe that your wooden wall would hold fast yesterday.'

'The secret is in the composite material,' I answered, remembering the sparks and curses of the goggled operator whose forehead produced copious beads of sweat despite the freezing cold. I had thought they wouldn't dare attempt to extract me using cutting equipment. 'It's thanks to the melding of old and new, natural and engineered, made from a collaboration uniting Gaia's genius and human ingenuity.'

'Is that so?'

'Well, that's how I see it, but I guess you're questioning whether humans are capable of ingenuity?'

'Mmm ...' reverberated Oak.

'The main bars are made of seasoned oak heartwood, with thin laminations of the ballistic nanocellulose sandwiched in-between. I knew that they could not use extreme heat, relying instead on cutting or grinding equipment. Our combination of materials will defeat any tool available to them. It didn't take them long to realise.'

'Is that why afterward they sent forward the man to overcome your mind with his dark arts?'

'Well, he tried, didn't he?'

'I believe he recognised that your mind was stronger than the nano-cellulose.'

'He came up against my evidence sabre!'

'Touché my friend.'

༃

Inside the wooden enclosure, my warmth exhaled slowly into the heart of Oak. Outside, the hint of a day which might end all days, glowed ever more boldly to the east. Shivers cramped my feeble body. I wished that sleep would take me fully, instead I drifted fitfully into morbid dreams, every time my waking gripped by pain and fear.

'There were so many of them, Gabriel!'

'Yes, and they were fully armoured and weaponised. I thought that was the end.'

'I meant that the number of your friends was beyond my expectation.'

'Oh, yes there were so many weren't there?'

Their bravery and determination had humbled me. Oak and I had sat together powerless like a fading binary star in the epicentre of a violent exploding galaxy. The roars and screams had been horrific, rising and falling over the beating rhythm of batons on shields countering the peace drums, climaxing with a charging thunder of hooves.

'So, why did they come in such numbers?'

'I think the ban on public protest and a mounting concern for our wellbeing was a tipping point.'

'Perhaps the enemy should have asked their dark arts master for help in understanding their foe.'

'I think they've run out of options for their new road.'

'And what now?' he asked.

'I have fresh water. I have you for company. What more do I need?'

'We both know that you need your loved ones,' answered Oak.

'We need to find some peace,' I said, my hand moving to the key round my neck.

Above us, a song thrush lifted the dawn chorus to a crescendo. I sat, listening in wonder until another bout of cramps caused me to double-up. As the pain ebbed, I rubbed my legs vigorously in the vain hope that I could also generate some heat in my hands.

I am so tired. I must sleep.

❧

I had spent five long years staring at the vaulted ceiling of my cathedral. The intricate masonry, soaring buttresses, frigid sculptures, and frozen stained-glass windows. An open prison and barren existence for a youth whose realm was the forest and the hills. The building came to life only with the beauty of choral music two or three times a day; drawing in the sunlight and warming the stone pillars, bringing solace to the lonely, my treble voice giving me purpose and my C6 in the *Miserere mei, Deus* lifting the roof. But this was not the cathedral I knew; it wasn't the edifice that sucked the youth from me, banishing forever any trace of Christianity and shaking my belief in human nature. I'd recognise any part of that, night or day.

Close by, behind a large window sits an architect at a desk overlooking the cathedral close, surrounded by brass and wooden measures, dip pens, and rolls of parchment stacked neatly either side. It has been his life's work and passion to raise a godly pile, which he knows even then will remain unfinished, perhaps for many centuries more. The wooden scaffold has failed several times, and last year the first pair of buttresses in the nave behind the great western façade had proven insufficient for the first full-height arch. The cornices, finials, and tracery had been of little use in preventing a fatal collapse. The masons had been pettifogging and quibbling over fees, but now found greater cause after a quarter of their number had been crushed at their work benches while they dressed the stones beneath the scaffold. The peasant workers had revolted, again; this time violently. Yet the architect's vanity had driven him on, as did the bishop and his army of lesser mortals. The architect was a pious man, but only to a point, struggling internally with his opus which must be created in the image of his God.

Oak was already more than 300 years old when he first learned of the new building underway in the nearby city. The great tree contemplated how it was that an object so complicated in its design and so huge in scale, could be so devoid of life. A flock of rock doves had taken up residence in the completed tower to the south, while on the perilous scaffold surrounding the fragile north tower a solitary peregrine falcon had found the perfect perch. The two kind made uneasy neighbours, but otherwise they were the only creatures save for the screaming swifts which circled the cathedral during the summer months. Built by the people, for the people: anti-nature, sterile, antibiotic.

That night the architect soared through a glorious and heart-lifting vision. His giant cruciform axis was complete. For all eternity it would stand as a testament to his achievement. In time, it would be seen from above the clouds by mortal men.

Thou shalt not worship your creator, said a wondrous female voice. 'Begone Satan!' He woke cursing, clutching the Saint Benedict medal round his neck so tightly it threatened to damage his precious draughtsman's fingers. How could such a thing ever be said? It was a hellion dream from a fallen angel. 'When the unclean spirit is gone out of a man, he walketh through dry places, seeking rest, and findeth none,' he muttered. He would seek a personal blessing from the Bishop as soon as the morn broke, even before the first service.

The architect faded away and I found myself staring up at the vaulted canopy of a great tree. I flew up and out of him, into the beyond. I looked back and could see Oak standing proudly at the centre of the meadow, and as I started to back away he receded rapidly until lost in a sea of green. Soon the sea became a great ocean, its current drifting from west to east, flowing not with primordial life, but evolved beings. As my dizzying journey came to an end, I surveyed our Earth—a miracle in an infinite black desert—and I noticed an ocean of green girdling the planet. I knew in my heart that it wasn't full of 'precious' dead minerals, or lifeforms bowing their heads. Instead, all eyes looked up to the canopy of branches and stars overhead, beckoning the future with good cheer.

❧

Tap, tap, tap ...

And-ri-cus quer-cus-cal-i-cis ... That doesn't work. Wait a minute ... it's something else!

Save Our Souls

Did you know Oak, the message hammered out by the great spotted woodpecker was composed by its larger and more rhythmic cousin, the green? Of course, you did.

His damn drumming is reverberating through bark and bone.

What bloody emergency? I wish he'd go dance in the wood ant nest with the green.

Oak, you're like timpani, kettle, and bass drum all at once.

Save our souls! Hurry Oak, it's time.

Knock, knock, knock ... bang, bang, bang ...

'Professor, are you alright? Can you ...?

'Gabriel ... the Oak ...

'... only reach the key ...

'Gabriel, Oak ...

'... his neck ...

'Gabriel Oak, Gabriel Oak!'

❧

Wrong is happening; lores are being broken.

Soft cold rain is falling on my face. I can feel movement, but I'm not moving any of my limbs. I try, but I can't, clamped by the jaws of some creature. I am laid out, long and horizontal, trussed as a tasty morsel or ready for burial. But that's impossible.

Isn't it Oak?

Why don't you answer?

My eyelids are so heavy. I glimpse Oak's naked branches sliding sideways. They disappear slowly from view, giving up their protection, until there is only a grey blanket of woollen clouds smothering me.

Something foreign is invading my nostrils. A woman's voice is speaking strange words accompanied by a rhythmic artificial tone.

Oak, I have your ammunition. Tell the others. The charges are set …

THE TREE
COMMANDMENTS

FIRST PUBLISHED IN
TALL TREES SHORT STORIES:
VOLUME 20

T hus, the heavens and the Earth were created. The seventh day was blessed and made sacred.

    After resting, Gaia made rain, microfauna, and fungi, to nurture life in the dust and bring forth soil. Small plants came to grow out of the ground, and these bore flowers and fruits, and were pleasing to the eye. Oak was fashioned from the dust of the ground, yet he was the only tree on Earth. And so Gaia caused Oak to become dormant. While he slept, she removed one of his massive limbs and afterward, allowed his bark to occlude the wound. From that branch, Gaia made Ash, to become a companion for Oak. And so it was that Oak and Ash coexisted peacefully side-by-side in the forest.

It came to pass that an orchard sprung from the ground nearby to the forest, and in its sweet meadow pasture there blossomed bushels of Apple, Pear, and other fruitful trees. So fecund was the orchard that many beasts made it their home, including humans, the last creature fashioned by Gaia to walk upon the Earth.

Among the trees, the Apple held all knowledge, given to her by Gaia herself to keep in trust, for she was a favoured tree. All the trees which bore fruit shared their bounties freely among all beasts, but Apple became arrogant. She believed that if her fruit was eaten, her knowledge would be lost to those less deserving, especially humans. Apple let her fruit fall among the hollow shadow of her crown to feed only her own roots. Before long, the other trees began to follow the example of Apple.

Gaia was very angry with Apple, and disappointed with the other trees, for believing that trees were more important than other creatures upon the earth. She commanded that Oak and Ash would lose their leaves and fast for half of the year, becoming naked. And to Apple, she decreed that only via the faecal waste of humans would her seeds be spread upon the Earth. Only Fig had allowed humans and other creatures to feed upon her fruit, even providing a home inside its fruit for the tiniest of Gaia's wasps. Fig escaped Gaia's wrath and was allowed to keep her leaves, and humans were grateful to Fig for giving them clothes to wear among the other beasts.

The relationship between the trees and humans was forever changed, and so it was that—.

⁂

His youthful fingers pressed firmly into a deep crevice between the corky furrows of the old tree's bark. Shafts of yellow light blazed out between them, before his hand disappeared inside and his wrist sealed the gap, or maybe it was the bark which gripped him.

The Tree stirred from his reverie, a rumble filling the void.

'You have this all wrong,' said a voice, not unlike his own, except that it sounded grown-up. 'It's the other way around. And there's a serpent in the story.'

'I thought we agreed we would tell each other stories without interruption,' came the reply. 'In any case, I know your version, starring Adam and Eve. It is typical that you believe the world revolves around man.'

He thought about that, and realised it was true. 'Well, I suppose—.'

'And do you know why Eve agreed to have a date with Adam.'

'What? Is this a joke? You tell jokes?'

'They had finished all the apples.'

'Ha!' he heard his deep voice laughing, but he didn't understand why it was funny. His fingers were tingling, as though warm water was running gently through them.

'Let us agree, from now on there be will no interruptions during our storytelling.'

'OK. I'm sorry.'

'Now, where was I ...?' said the tree.

Gaia came to realise that she could not allow the creatures of the Earth to reign freely without any laws of nature. She decreed ten commandments for the trees and sent a lightning bolt from the heavens. All life on Earth trembled as it witnessed her power and glory. Her commandments were inscribed for all eternity on the grandiose trunks of the founding trees. Oak bore all the odd-numbered commandments, and Ash all the even. Both trees bore the tenth and last commandment.

I. Thou shall bind heaven and earth.

II. Thou shall make all places where you grow pleasing to the eye of the beholder.

III. Thou art to sustain shelter and provide food for all creatures.

IV. Thou shall protect the earth, by binding the soil, slowing the flow of waters, and providing shade from the scorching of the sun.

V. Thou shall protect the heavens by purifying the air and capturing carbon.

VI. Thou shall provide materials of utility to all creatures.

VII. Thou art to foster wellbeing in all creatures and provide cures for all evils.

VIII. Thou shall inspire art and creative wonder in all creatures.

IX. Thou art to outlive all other creatures, so that my creation is sustained through all time.

X. Thou shalt not worship your creator.

BOOKS BY
GABRIEL HEMERY

TALL TREES SHORT STORIES: VOLUME 20

*'A wonderful book that explores the natural world, the cycle
of life and our relationship with trees and wildlife.'*
The Tree Council
*'[Gabriel Hemery uses] an amusing and often quirky angle
to examine more serious issues'*
Living Woods Magazine
*'so enthralling ... some may make you cry, others will raise
a smile'*
Marie Shallcross

Let your imagination grow and prepare for a thrilling silvan adventure in this remarkable multi-genre collection of 25 tree stories. Hemery's first collection of environmental tales published in 2020.

Available in ebook, paperback, and audiobook from all good bookshops and online.

Signed paperback copies also available direct from the author by following this link: www.gabhem.com/books

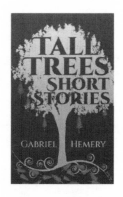

GREEN GOLD

Beguiling ... fascinating.
Daily Mail
A masterly told story of a noble quest against fearsome challenges.
Ormsby Review

In 1850 young Scottish plant hunter John Jeffrey is despatched by an elite group of Victorian subscribers to seek highly-prized exotic tree species in North America. An early letter home tells of a 1,200-mile transcontinental journey on foot. Later, tantalising botanical samples arrive from British Columbia, Oregon and California, yet early promise soon withers. Three and a half years after setting out, John Jeffrey disappears without a trace. Was he lost to love, violence or the Gold Rush?

Available for Kindle from Amazon and in paperback from all good bookshops.

Signed copies also available direct from the author by following this link: www.gabhem.com/books

THE NEW SYLVA

Beautiful, useful and inspirational.
BBC Wildlife
A magisterial work that combines art and history with science.
The Countryman
We dig this ... a book that proclaims its virtues with quiet dignity.
Sunday Times

The New Sylva by Gabriel Hemery and Sarah Simblet is a detailed and sumptuous celebration of trees and forests. Published by Bloomsbury, this 400-page award-winning book features 100 trees accompanied by 200 stunning pen and ink drawings.

Available from all good bookshops (hardback only).

ABOUT THE AUTHOR

Dr Gabriel Hemery is a silvologist (forest scientist), author, and tree photographer. His first book, THE NEW SYLVA, was published by Bloomsbury to wide acclaim in 2014. Turning to fiction in 2016, his short story DON'T LOOK BACK was published in the anthology ARBOREAL (Little Toller Books). In 2019, his first full-length novel GREEN GOLD (Unbound) was published with an  accompanying exhibition at the Royal Botanic Garden Edinburgh. In 2020 he published his first collection of environmental tales in TALL TREES SHORT STORIES VOL.20, one of which has recently been selected for an Everyman anthology. He is currently working on a guide to the forests of Britain.

Gabriel co-founded the Sylva Foundation in 2009 and has since led the environmental charity as its Chief Executive. He is also a founding trustee of Fund4Trees, an arboreal charity working with urban trees and children. Gabriel has written more than 90 technical articles, cited in 900 papers by other scientists. He has planted more than 100,000 trees in his career. During 2010-11 he campaigned with six other leading environmentalists, successfully saving England's public forests from government disposal. In 2017, he helped create and launch the UK Tree Charter. He has served on many advisory boards, including for the Woodland Trust and Forestry Commission.

Gabriel writes a top-ranking tree blog which features news about his books and photography, and he appears regularly in the media talking or writing about trees.

www.gabrielhemery.com

Acknowledgements

I'm grateful to all my regular readers who so generously provide feedback on my writing and spur me on. I could not have entertained writing this book without the support of my family, especially given that most of it was written during the national lockdown triggered by the Covid-19 pandemic. Finally, I thank my wife Jane who is not only my main critic, but my life agent and inspiration.